Road to Europe

ROAD TO EUROPE

by Ferdinand Oyono

Translated from the French
by Richard Bjornson

An Original from Three Continents

©1989 Richard Bjornson

First English-language edition

Three Continents Press
1636 Connecticut Avenue, N.W.
Washington, D.C. 20009

First published as *Chemin d'Europe,* Paris: Julliard, 1960

Library of Congress Cataloging-in-Publication Data:

Oyono, Ferdinand, 1929–
    Road to Europe
    Translation of: Chemin d'Europe
    I. Title.
PQ3989.09C513 1989 843 86-51301
ISBN 0-89410-590-6
ISBN 0-89410-591-4 (pbk.)

Cover art by Max K. Winkler
©Three Continents Press, 1989

Contents

Introduction

Ferdinand Oyono's first two novels—*Houseboy* and *The Old Man and the Medal*—have become classics of modern African literature. Taught as examples of anti-colonialist literature in schools and universities throughout Africa, Europe, and America, they have been read by millions of people, and critics have devoted numerous commentaries to them. Oyono's third novel, *Road to Europe,* has not received nearly the same attention. This is unfortunate for several reasons. *Houseboy* and *The Old Man and the Medal* are humorous, relatively straightforward narratives that depict the tragic disillusionment of naive Africans who seek to become "somebody" in colonialist society by adopting roles conceived for them by Europeans. Both the houseboy Toundi and the old man Meka are victims of a cruel system, because they allow themselves to be duped by the promises it holds out to them. The way in which their own good faith is betrayed reveals the human consequences of colonialist oppression and serves as an indictment of the unjust system.

In contrast, *Road to Europe* is a highly complex narrative in which the central character, Barnabas, is neither the center of human value nor the dupe of a cruel and unjust system. He is simply an intelligent African who, having internalized the rules of the game in colonialist society, decides to become "somebody" by playing according to them. Yet, although he attains the goal he has set for himself, he is victimized in a more profound sense than either Toundi or Meka. Whereas their pride temporarily blinds them to the truth about themselves and their relations to others, his calculated individualism permanently isolates him from any genuine human contact with Europeans or fellow Africans. *Road to Europe* provides a penetrating insight into the nature of this corrupt mentality. At the same time, it is Oyono's most mature work, characterized by an extraordinary verbal dexterity and filled with caricatural portraits that bear comparison with those of classic European writers such as Voltaire, La Bruyère,

1

Quevedo, and Swift. The humor, the anticolonialist stance, and the deep sense of humanity in Oyono's earlier novels also emerge in *Road to Europe,* but they must be discovered behind the screen of a less-than-admirable narrator's consciousness. Readers who make the effort to penetrate this screen will be rewarded by gaining access to a remarkable novel that probes the roots of corruption in the colonized mind and displays the author's dazzling mastery over the resources of language.

The socio-cultural context in which all of Oyono's novels take place is essentially similar, and each of his major characters confronts the same basic dilemma. In the colonialist situation, Africans were offered the choice between two equally unsatisfactory systems of value: they could identify with traditional African customs, or they could seek to assimilate European modes of thought and behavior. Both alternatives were untenable. Although traditional society fostered many decent values like communal solidarity, hospitality, a celebratory sense of life, and an acceptance of human limitations in the face of implacable natural forces, it had proved incapable of preserving itself when challenged by the technological superiority and formal organizational skills of the European colonizers. Furthermore, traditional attitudes were often unjust and inefficacious in the sense that they were based on outmoded superstitions and authoritarian social hierarchies. In many cases, traditional attitudes had become so distorted within the colonialist context that they led to patently ridiculous forms of behavior.

But the possibility of assimilating European values hardly offered colonized Africans a legitimate opportunity to escape the restraints placed upon them by a traditional world-view. Based upon the unquestioned assumption of white superiority, the dominant European ideology in the colonies promulgated the stereotyped notion that Africans were either childlike or barbarous. For this reason, Africans were supposed to recognize their inherent inferiority and accommodate themselves to European schemes for establishing a "civilized" order in their part of the world. By acquiescing in such assumptions, Africans presumably earned the good will of benevolent mentors, who in turn rewarded them with perquisites that were associated with the European way of life. In reality, of course, the colonialist rhetoric was a hypocritically self-serving lie. Africans were not inferior to Europeans, and the latter were less than interested in "civilizing" the former than in realizing a profit for themselves.

By inculcating Africans with a sense of their own inferiority, however, they could be subjected to a system of unequal exchange in which they actually gave Europeans much more than they ever received in return. Because there was a latent awareness of the hypocrisy inherent in this situation, both Europeans and Africans tended to don false masks in their dealings with each other—the Europeans promoting their self-interest and disguising their anxieties beneath a facade of disdain and arbitrary cruelty, the Africans preserving their own physical well-being and camouflaging their resentment behind blandly smiling faces. The gulf between the races became virtually unbridgeable under such circumstances, and the ensuing atmosphere was pervaded with mistrust. This is the environment in which all Oyono's principal characters face the impossible task of defining themselves when neither traditional values nor colonialist ideology offer them a viable basis for forging a stable sense of identity.

Oyono's novels are invariably set in the Bulu country of South-Central Cameroon near Ebolowa, where he himself grew up and went to school, and the world view behind them bears some resemblance to the one embedded in Bulu oral tales like those of Kulu the tortoise, who copes with an inexorably harsh world of power relationships by resorting to ruses that are often quite cruel. There is no direct relationship between goodness and reward or evil and punishment in these tales, and the victims of Kulu's ruses generally lose the advantage of their superior physical strength when they succumb to illusions that are sustained by their own gullibility and pride. The moral of these tales revolves around the dual recognition that all creatures exist in a world governed by the interplay of competing forces and that those who adopt a false interpretation of reality render themselves vulnerable to exploitation by others. Similarly, in Oyono's novels, people who accept Christian myths at face value, naively expecting to receive their merited rewards, are fools, susceptible to being manipulated by Europeans and summarily dismissed when their usefulness is at an end. They also isolate themselves from the African community that has traditionally nourished its members in both physical and psychological terms, but most importantly they place themselves in a situation where they will ultimately have to confront the denial of their own humanity.

Traditional society does not provide them with a viable alternative to this psychological dead end, because it is generally represented by decrepit old men who use it as a pretext for monopolizing the power, prestige, wealth, and women still available to Africans under European domination. According to Oyono, both traditional and colonialist systems are artificial constructions. Beneath any role people might play in them, they continue to live like animals in the sense that they still eat, urinate, defecate, make love, suffer, and die in a world that is ugly and dirty. Within the compass of Oyono's fictional universe, there is no solution to the dilemma of the impossible choice. He merely establishes an ironic perspective by means of which readers can gain insight into a perverse situation and form their own opinions about it.

In *Houseboy* and *The Old Man and the Medal,* the impact of this perspective upon the reader is posited upon a realization that the protago-

nists are more than the stereotypes imposed upon them by French colonialists. Although Toundi and Meka may well be dupes of the system and
their own blindness toward its hypocrisy, their suffering and humiliation
bear witness to their humanity, which, once acknowledged, becomes an
implicit refutation of the colonialist ideology. In the painful clash between
their dream of future happiness and their experience of a harsh reality
that denies it to them, they eventually relinquish their illusions, although
by that time they can but recognize their existential solitude in a harsh,
unforgiving universe. *Road to Europe* functions in an entirely different
fashion, for Aki Barnabas is a young Cameroonian who actually realizes
his dream of going to France, where, more than a year after leaving his
homeland, he records the story of his "success." But like many fictive
autobiographers, he inadvertently reveals his own shame and weakness
while boasting about his accomplishment. The primary standard of value
in Oyono's third novel is not the protagonist's humanity, as it was in his
earlier works, but rather the humanity that he had suppressed within himself in order to achieve his goal.

In an interview several years after the publication of *Road to Europe,*
Oyono asserted that Barnabas' culture "enabled him to become a man
like everyone else." But "everyone else" is hardly admirable. The name
"Barnabas" echoes that of the criminal whom the people of Jerusalem
chose to free instead of Christ. By selecting such a name, Oyono is sug-
gesting that his protagonist's success is by no means a reward for his right-
eousness but rather a reflection of the universal cynicism that permits
thieves to go free, while good men suffer. In fact, Barnabas owes his
presence in Europe primarily to the fact that he can, on the spur of the
moment, render a convincing account of his own salvation, a task for
which he had been well prepared by an earlier stint in the Catholic
seminary.

Near the end of the novel, he relates how he stumbled upon a revivalist meeting where Africans were publicly confessing their sins. Seeing
the well-fed "niggers" on the stage and knowing that he can fabulate
better stories than those he had just heard, Barnabas seized his chance: "I
was going to amaze that screaming crowd with my story. What a novel my
life!" At this point, his primary goal was to achieve an effect that would
allow him to obtain the passionately desired trip to Europe. As he approaches one of the white organizers of the meeting, the first sentence of
his tale occurs to him—the sentence that would open "the road to
Europe" to him. Since the title of the novel echoes this phrase, it is quite
possible to link its opening words—"I had lost my voice"—with the words
Barnabas utters at the revivalist meeting. Whether or not the novel re-
capitulates the story he told that night, it clearly contains the same
materials and reflects a similar set of motivations.

In relating the events of his past life, Barnabas undoubtedly hopes to project a favorable image of himself. For example, in the few comments he makes about his present situation in France, he seems to be explaining what might be regarded by others as flaws in his character. In case readers might notice his tendency to distance himself from the suffering of others, he admits that he has always had a lively sense of the ridiculous. Although his actual circumstances differ considerably from those of his youth, he declares, "I still have a certain sense of humor in the face of real or imaginary sufferings, a trait that has often caused people to look upon me as a frivolous, amoral being." Such a statement implies that he actually considers himself neither frivolous nor amoral, even though others may interpret his actions in this sense. Within the larger framework of his story, the narrating Barnabas wants readers to see him as an individual who overcame obstacles and frustrations to achieve his goal in a corrupt society. "Poor, without relatives or friends, and ridiculed for my dreams, I would not, however, allow myself to be discouraged," he boasts at one point. "I must confess that I was . . . a monster of optimism in a country where man had been dehumanized by the appetite for power and profit and by the cult of selfishness." In the first place, his self-characterization is not entirely accurate. He did have relatives, and his education at the seminary enabled him to hold several jobs during a time when the majority of his countrymen were unemployed. In the second place, many of the traits he ascribes to his environment can also be found in himself. In such passages, he is overstating the difficulties he faced in order to predispose readers in his favor.

Yet behind the narrating Barnabas is the implicit presence of the author who created him and the series of verbal clues by means of which readers can discern the less positive aspects of the character who is ostensibly presenting a veracious account of his own life. Barnabas has not been duped by the colonialist ideology in the same way as Toundi and Meka had been. In contrast to them, he realizes that the European's promises of friendship and future happiness are fraudulent. However, rather than condemning the cynical attitude of the colonialist, he internalizes them and determines to conform to them in as calculated a fashion as possible. Also, he cannot completely disguise his resentment against those who mocked his aspirations while he was still, as he says, painfully seeking his way in life. Publishing the story of his "success" constitutes one way of avenging himself upon them. At various points, he himself hints at the self-pity or the morbid obsession with money that he shared with his mother, and he repeatedly reveals his incapacity to trust and love other people. Barnabas' mentality is thus a highly complex product of the society in which he is living. In fact, the very existence of such a mentality constitutes a penetrating commentary on the perverse nature of the society that engendered it.

Filtered through the distortions and self-serving projections of the fictive narrator's consciousness, the story itself details the evolution of that consciousness. It answers the question: how could someone become what the narrating Barnabas has become? Like Toundi, the young Barnabas formulates a vision of future happiness based on a rebellion against his father's tyranny and a yearning for the comfort of a European life style. The basis for the mentality in which this vision takes shape is initially forged in the tense relationship that imprisons his mother, his father, and himself. Seen through the eyes of the narrating Barnabas, the father is a ludicrous figure—a hunch-backed "old nigger," whose ignorance was compounded by a simple-minded devotion to the Catholic faith. Having become a gardener for the priests at the local mission, he enrolled his son at their school in the hope that the boy would someday become a priest. But even at such an early age, Barnabas resented the old man's desire to enhance his own stature by identifying with the accomplishments of a talented son. It galled him that his father took pleasure in his academic successes; he in turn exasperated his father with his mocking sense of humor and his resistance to endless rounds of daily prayer.

The split between them became definitive after Barnabas left the seminary, dashing the old man's most cherished dream. In one sense, the narrating Barnabas gains revenge upon his father by depicting him as a grotesque buffoon. Even in recounting the old man's death, Barnabas emphasizes the comic aspects of the funeral: the corpse rolled from side to side on its hunchback, and the coffin was weighted with rocks to make it sink into the water-filled grave. In another sense, Barnabas reveals the extent to which his own personality has been shaped by a resentment against his father and by his own shame at the thought of being associated with such a man. His interpretation of the relationship becomes obvious in the way he attributes meaning to an accidental occurence at the funeral, for when the coffin sank into the grave, a spurt of water shot up and hit Barnabas in the face. The narrator describes the gush of water as a "slap in the face." One of the primary motivations in Barnabas' youth was a desire to liberate himself from the control of a father he disliked, to dissociate himself completely from him, and to avoid resembling him in any way.

One expression of this desire is his attachment to his mother, whom he describes as the opposite of his father. She was young, beautiful, and extraordinarily resourceful in practical matters. Like many other women in Oyono's novels, she possessed an inner strength and perspicaciousness that most of the men lack. She was the one who sustained Barnabas in his moments of weakness. He in turn wanted to make her happy and draw her away from his father. He recalls her moments of joyous laughter when they walked through the fields and forests together, and he regrets having been unable to sustain the momentary pleasure he had given her when he took her to see a French movie. At one point she actually abandoned her husband in order to live with him. Even as a full-grown man, he remained so attached to her that he feels incapable of loving any other woman, for in his eyes she was "the only woman one can ever love without resentment, the only woman one never forgets." This attitude harmed Barnabas in two ways: it prevented him from enjoying any other kind of female companionship, and it rendered him dependent on her emotional support. Whenever he felt sorry for himself, he cried on her shoulder. Whenever he needed assurance of his own self worth or absolution from his feelings of guilt, he turned to her. Although she eventually went back to her husband when Barnabas began to drink excessively, she returned after the old man's death and became the primary support for Barnabas' image of himself.

She was the one who seized upon his fantasy of going to France and made it seem possible. For him, the idea had originally been nothing more than a daydream; for her, it was a goal to be achieved by practical efforts—obtaining money from the tribal elders, writing to the French authorities, or painstakingly saving money from the profits of a small harki business she had started for the purpose. If Barnabas lacked resolve, it was at least in part because he had learned that he could always turn to his mother for moral and physical support. This pattern of dependency reemerges in his subsequent schemes, for they all depend on his ability to convince others to do for him what he cannot do for himself. If his adult mentality is tinged with the cynical opportunism behind the colonialist ideology, he has been prepared to embrace this attitude by his ambivalent relationship to his parents—attachment to a loving but strong-willed, overly protective mother and rebellion against a father who had been duped by the colonialist rhetoric and the Christian mythology that sanctioned it.

Barnabas' first three experiences outside the home placed him in roles which reflect major aspects of the myth of European superiority: religion, commerce, and romantic love. Each of them is based on illusory appearances, but rather than falling victim to their false promises, Barnabas assimilated the self-serving attitudes behind them. From the beginning he was skeptical about religion. During his first communion, for example, he failed to experience the revelation that other children seemed to be undergoing. He felt only the urge to vomit because he knew that the host, far from being inhabited by the Holy Spirit, had actually been prepared by the unclean hands of a syphilitic, apostate Moslem. When he agreed to enter the seminary, his choice was an expedient for gaining entry into the forbidden paradise of knowledge in the hope of eventually acquiring a civil service position that would exempt him from the harsh conditions imposed upon most Africans. He himself refers to his decision as the "Trojan horse of a religious vocation." During his seven years at the seminary, however, he did become accustomed to European culture—its books, its music, and its material comforts.

He also developed an intimate friendship with a sensitive Gabonese mulatto, and the priests eventually expelled him from the seminary for reasons of suspected homosexuality. The narrating Barnabas denies the charge, but his descriptions of the relationship are sufficiently ambiguous to leave some doubt about what actually occurred, and his later comments about other male characters hint at an undercurrent of homoeroticism in his personality—a rather rare motif in African fiction. In any case, Barnabas was the dominant partner in his relationship with the mulatto, who had, he boasts, become "my thing." Whether or not the priests' suspicions were justified, they placed Barnabas under a cloud of shame. His response was to become obsessed with a desire to avenge himself upon the seminary director while maintaining a facade of respectable innocence in front of the townspeople who bombarded him with indiscreet questions. The seminary experience established what subsequently became a recurrent pattern in Barnabas' life. After donning a mask to deceive others into giving him what he wants, he either loses patience with his role or proves too weak to carry it out resolutely. To avoid blaming himself for the ensuing failure, he directs his resentment against others and seeks to maintain the appearance of injured innocence.

By the time Barnabas left the seminary, he had also abandoned his desire to become a civil servant, since he had come to regard positions in the colonial administration as demeaning. What he now wanted was an opportunity to "realize himself." Because he believed this opportunity existed in the commercial sector, he took advantage of his reputation as a former seminarian to obtain a post as solicitor for the Greek merchant Kriminopoulos. His employer's name evokes the fundamentally dishonest nature of a typical colonialist enterprise—buying agricultural produce as cheaply as possible from peasants and selling manufactured goods back to them at exorbitant prices. Although Barnabas apparently experiences some success as an intermediary in this "criminal" business, he could not take his role seriously and abandoned his job on a farcical whim. Yet he had learned something. Like the Catholic church, Kriminopoulos' business succeeds by convincing gullible people to believe in false appearances. Barnabas himself could not believe in them, but he clearly perceived the advantage of being among the deceivers rather than among the deceived. From this point on, his plans were never completely free from a spirit of calculated, materialistic self-interest.

Thus, when he accepted a position as private tutor to the eight-year-old daughter of an expatriate Frenchman who neglected his wife in favor of numerous African mistresses, Barnabas explained to his mother that he was not concerned with the private affairs of white men. All he wanted was for them to help him, because "they by themselves owned the largest share of the world's wealth." This spirit of calculation, however, is mediated by the literary texts he had read during his European-style education at the seminary. In his own mind, he became like Julien Sorel, the young and ambitious hero of Stendhal's *The Red and the Black,* and the spurned Madame Gruchet became his Madame de Rènal. The situation is rendered even more complex than its literary precedent by the fact that Madame Gruchet also represents the unattainable white woman and symbolically incarnates France, the country he had been conditioned to admire since his earliest childhood. "She fascinated me, titillated me with all the Romantic associations of the forbidden white woman," he declares, fantasizing about how her husband might grant her a divorce and send them both to France.

The irony is that all these comparisons and wish dreams existed only in Barnabas' mind. He was not a romantic hero, and Madame Gruchet did not love him the way Madame de Rènal had loved Julien Sorel. On one occasion she did seem to reveal a passion for him by throwing her arms around his neck, pressing her body against his, and weeping uncontrollably. Although he was astonished and immediately interpreted her actions within the context of his wish-dream, he soon realized that she had merely been venting her anxiety over a sick daughter's high fever. The contrast between Barnabas' literature-inspired version of reality and the actual situation is comic, but it is also tragic insofar as it reflects the void and self-hatred he senses inside himself. At one point he thought she might help him forget "the dreadful feeling of emptiness," and although he desired to take the suffering woman in his arms and comfort her, he was prevented from doing so by "a feeling of impurity that was so viscous and sticky that it made me disgusted with myself." Beneath Barnabas' self-dramatization lurks the fear and shame that undermine the romantic role he has imagined for himself. In fact, the role itself is merely one of the many psychological ploys he adopted to avoid confronting the reality about himself.

His mother recognized the futility of his romantic project from the beginning. She wept at the prospect of his certain frustration, called him "poor Barnabas," and asked him how he could play "such an ignoble farce" on them. To her it seemed far more practical to solicit funds from the tribal elders, who might be willing to support his study abroad in the expectation that he would later return home and "be somebody" in whom the entire tribe could take pride. The difficulty with her plan is twofold: the elders were degenerate old men with little interest in fostering the careers of young people who might challenge their undeserved privileges, and

Barnabas himself was too ashamed of his association with them to humble himself in their presence. This latent conflict surfaced when he cursed under his breath, for his lack of respect doomed in advance any chance of obtaining the desired support.

Although Barnabas is partly responsible for the failure of the mission, the visit to Fimsten Vavap provides Oyono with an opportunity to include traditional society in his panorama of the social types that inhabit the chaotic world where Barnabas is seeking his way. Vavap and the elders claim to be the true inheritors of a great and noble past, and they accuse the younger generation of disturbing the natural harmony which had previously existed between the tribe and nature. In reality, Vavap is an ugly old man with a herniated navel and flies hovering around his encrusted eyes. He regards all women, including Barnabas' mother, as his rightful property, yet he makes no productive contribution to the life of the community, remaining content to live from the work of others, like the poor woman Barnabas glimpsed struggling beneath a heavy burden she was carrying from the fields while her husband lounged lazily in his compound. Even if Barnabas could have controlled his disgust, it is obvious that traditional society offers him no viable alternative to the distorted sense of identity that has begun to crystallize in him.

Barnabas' next position as official guide for the self-styled Africa experts staying at the Hôtel de France was undoubtedly a more appropriate response to the prevailing commercial atmosphere in the country. After losing his job with the Gruchets, he had initially passed the time by strolling around the market, somewhat like the African prostitutes who ambled about the hotel in the hope of enticing white customers. When it became apparent that his education would enable him to act as an intermediary for the self-styled experts, the hotel proprietor hired him on an official basis. Again like the prostitutes, he spent his time waiting for white customers, to whom he held out the promise of exotic sights and experiences. With his principal customer, the French anthropologist Cimetierre, he demonstrated how well he had learned to mask his true feelings in conforming to the white man's expectations of him. Whenever Cimetierre sermonized about African customs, Barnabas dutifully responded, "Oh, master, it's magnificent!" In retrospect, the narrating Barnabas mocks the pseudo-knowledge of such experts and the reputations they make for themselves in Europe, but since he felt no attachment to traditional values, he had no compunction about playing the role of a "good-natured, continually smiling native" in order to profit from their pretentious misconstruals of his society.

At about the same time Barnabas began his career as a "prostitute" for the Africa experts, he entered into his first affair with a woman. In response to the self-pity and self-disgust he had felt in the presence of his mother and the unattainable Madame Gruchet, he courted Anatatchia, the "least indomitable" of the prostitutes who gathered nightly in front of the Hôtel de France. However, she insisted upon initiating him into the bizarre love-making techniques of her favorite white lover, and when he objected, she threw his pants into the courtyard. The incident constituted a real humiliation, for it showed that even the lowest prostitute could disdain his attentions. He himself continued to spy on Anatatchia from behind trees and houses, but he never again approached her directly. Rather than the romantic hero he would like to be, he was no more than a failed lover who refused to look inside himself for the causes of his failure.

His relationship with Anatatchia did place him in intimate contact with another person who saw and judged him, but because he could not bear to face her image of him, he fled from her glance and from the knowledge that her opinions were circulating in the town. When she threw his pants into the courtyard, he worried more about the possibility that others might witness his disgrace than about the fact of his humiliation. And when she appeared during one of his sessions in Cimetierre's room, he suddenly saw her as a "frightful monument to my lost time." At this moment, he developed such a "violent nausea for everything" that he rushed madly into the night. The narrating Barnabas' description of the scene is highly ambiguous, for he does not specify the reason for his disgust. He may be referring to the time he lost in pursuing Anatatchia, but he may equally well be alluding to the time he had lost serving as an official guide for the pseudo-experts. Both he and Anatatchia were in Cimetierre's room for the same purpose; they were both "prostitutes" who took money for finding ways of pleasing a white man. The situation and Barnabas' disgust becomes even more ambivalent when readers recall the hints of his homosexual tendencies at the seminary. In any case, it is obvious that Anatatchia's presence made it impossible for him to repress his profound sense of shame. As a result, he ran away from her to avoid looking into himself.

The following morning he even quit his job, and later his own worst fears were realized, when he accidentally overheard Anatatchia gossiping with a group of women at the river. She mocked her former lover's intentions of going to Europe and "becoming somebody," his love-making, his constant questioning, and his disdain for the other people of the town. She asserted that he had "delusions of grandeur like all those men who have been deprived of women for too long" and predicted that he would end his days in prison. There was certainly an element of truth in her appraisal of Barnabas—he does have delusions of grandeur, and the weakness of character does stem from an over-reliance on his mother— but he was less concerned with learning the truth about himself than with repressing his shame. Before the women's conversation ended, he had already left the scene because he could not bear the thought that others were mocking him behind his back. In fact, it was this thought that convinced him to depart from the town, for he could hardly take himself seriously, if he knew that everyone else was laughing at him, and he desperately wanted to take himself seriously.

Ironically, his aspirations were taken seriously by people who did not know him. On the bus to Y——, where he was going to pursue a government scholarship that would enable him to study in France, his fellow passengers learned of his projected journey and showered him with money. Their bank notes expressed a characteristic African generosity and sense of solidarity, but they also reflected the naiveté and gullibility that rendered Africans vulnerable to being duped by the colonialist myth. The passengers wanted to see him in the role of hero and savior—precisely the role he had conceived for himself. In fact, when he had written letters for others in the market place, he had always concluded with a phrase that identified him as the people's "savior" who had been unjustly dismissed from the seminary. On the bus, the passengers dreamed that a man like Barnabas could travel to the white man's country, marry a white woman, and become a commandant. "That'll change a lot of things for us in this country!" exclaimed an old woman, and a male nurse exhorted him: "Come back and save us like Moses saved the children of Israel from the bondage of Egypt!" These simple people gave him what the elders of his own tribe had refused, and yet they were investing in a chimera. Although Barnabas had no assurance he would ever actually go to France, he cynically pocketed their contributions and ultimately lost a portion of it while running from a group of angry white men. The passengers' generosity proved futile, but from the very beginning it had been based on a hopelessly naive expectation of what Barnabas could achieve for them. Yet the experience did reinforce a lesson he had already learned under various guises: the world is divided into deceivers and deceived, and it is better to be among the deceivers. Now he also realized that it was far easier to deceive those who did not know him—those who failed to suspect what lie beneath his mask.

The absurdity of the passengers' image of Barnabas is underscored by the white colonial administrator's refusal to grant him a scholarship for study in France. More than seven months earlier Barnabas had written a grandiloquent twenty-page letter to the authorities. Already at that time he had envisioned himself on board a ship that would take him to the "only country where I can 'realize' myself." When he received no reply from the government, he became convinced that the postal clerk was keeping it from him. In a paranoid fashion, he follows the unsuspecting clerk home from work in the hope of overhearing some reference to the anxiously awaited response. In reality, the government had no intention of granting him a scholarship, and like the romanticization of his relationship with Madame Gruchet, the plot of a devious postal employee existed only in his own mind. It was a way to avoid recognizing that his dream had no basis in fact.

However, once he had spoken with Dansette, the colonial administrator, he could no longer lie to himself. In both his letter and his personal plea to Dansette, he posed as an enthusiastic booster of French civilization and culture. Indeed, his praise was so exaggerated that he himself feared for a moment that Dansette might have him thrown into prison for his effrontery. But, accustomed to the clichés of the colonialist myth, the Frenchman seemed not to notice how calculatedly Barnabas used them. He merely saw a black man old enough to start a family and counseled him to be reasonable and learn a trade. Barnabas did not want to hear such advice, but he was powerless to contest it, unless he could act well enough to persuade others to give him what he wanted. In this case, his act failed.

During his conversation with Dansette, Barnabas was subjected to the stereotyped thinking of white colonialists. Although deeply disappointed by his failure to obtain a trip to France, he remained indifferent to the fact that his interlocutor viewed him in reifying terms. In fact, Barnabas was quite willing to play the role of the assimilated African as a means of obtaining his desired goal. Unlike Meka and Toundi, he had no vested psychological interest in the false appearances of the colonialist rhetoric.

Yet his sickness is deeper than theirs because he has internalized the cynical, exploitative attitude beneath this rhetoric. Only on two occasions was he obliged to acknowledge a fleeting awareness of the existential solitude that Meka and Toundi experience. The first occurred after Madame Gruchet slammed the door of her villa in his face. All alone in the mud and rain, he lamented, "I suddenly tasted the bilious pleasure of feeling the profound sensation of who I really was." This insight into his solitary existence as a black man whose humanity had just been denied by the colonialist mentality was fleeting and unpleasant. He succeeded in repressing it because he had learned to regard himself as a manipulator of appearances rather than as the gullible victim of them.

Later, he experienced a similar brief moment of awareness at a European nightclub in Y——. He had met the middle-aged shrimp salesman Bendjanga-Boy on the bus; after his disappointing interview with Dansette, his drunken tribesman reappeared and invited him into the back seat of a huge American automobile he had hired for the occasion. Having concluded that life is brief and susceptible to being terminated at any moment, Bendjanga-Boy had decided to squander all his money on a single night of living like a white man. Because Barnabas no longer had any plans, he passively accepted the invitation and accompanied the older man into the nightclub. There he felt a roomful of hostile eyes staring at him. As in the case of Madame Gruchet, he could neither ignore their disdain nor suppress the intense sensation of existing as a solitary black man in a white-dominated environment. On this occasion the real-world consequences of the white man's reductionist image of the black man became evident in an outburst of rage when Bendjanga-Boy told the owner he wanted to make love to a white woman. After the interlopers were unceremoniously (and symbolically) thrown on the refuse bins outside the establishment, a drunken crowd of white men poured out of the nightclub, shouting obscenities at the two "apes" and hinting about the possibilities of lynching them. The scene provides a dramatic illustration of the way in which black humanity is routinely denied by adherents of the colonialist mythology.

Yet despite the fact that Barnabas ran for his life to avoid becoming the victim of this stereotyped image of blackness, he readily caught his breath, composed himself, and told his story at the revivalist meeting—the story that finally procured him a ticket to France. His chameleon-like change and his repression of the human feelings he had just been obliged to confront were only possible because he had assimilated the mentality behind the colonialist ideology. Like the Europeans in Africa, the narrating Barnabas succeeds in overlooking all evidence that contradicts his favorable self-image. What he does not realize is that, in vaunting his success, he is actually condemning himself. And the recognition of this fact provides readers with the key that unlocks the complex artistry of Oyono's highly provocative *Road to Europe*.

Richard Bjornson
Columbus, Ohio, 1986

Road to Europe

One

I had lost my voice, as I did at the beginning of every afternoon when the heat has cleared the streets of natives who had come in from the bush and when the boss, his belly crushed against the protruding drawer of the cash register, had fallen asleep . . . .

At the time I was a salesman, or rather a solicitor, in the shop of Monsieur Kriminopoulos, who had stationed me not behind the counter, but outside, abandoning me to the furious outbreaks of foul weather in my part of the country and condemning me to daily sentry duty in the middle of the filthy dead-end street on which our store was located.

I owed this job to my youth and my reputation as a former seminarian—a reputation convincingly sustained by the intellectual appanage of my glasses.

I can see myself at the seminary—how far I am now from that little Barnabas! Time and the rigors of life had distanced me from him . . . and I ask myself if it was really me. Yet no matter how strange it seems to me now, I feel attached to that period; it is a part of me that experienced a sort of life which no longer exists and which bears no resemblance at all to my present state of existence, except insofar as I still have a certain sense of humor in the face of real or imaginary sufferings, a trait that has often caused people to look upon me as a frivolous, amoral being. This lively taste for whimsy, an absolute standard against which I measure all things, was the despair of my father, a pious old fellow who was always ready to box one's ears. The poor man believed he had sired one of God's elect, and nothing could shake his faith in this pertinacious idea; he had the dogged persistence of a gold prospector who had flaired the trace of a nugget, and although my mother was upset by the idea, she remained a prisoner of the fear her husband inspired in her, for she was often afraid he would avenge himself upon me . . . .

Papa had suffered a great deal because of his ignorance. The victim of

17

foolish pride, he was revolted, despite the reproofs of my mother, by the thought of enrolling in adult-education courses, sitting among women, and stumbling through recitations like a child. In the end, he compromised and alleged his ardent faith as a pretext for devoting himself to the Catholic religion, which succeeded in degrading him completely. He abandoned the night-watchman's position he had held in the service of a Greek merchant, and with the passage of time, a hump of misery grew between his shoulders, gradually piercing through his old khaki jacket and reducing the spot around it to a film of lint. He would have liked for us to pray endlessly, to transform each instant of leisure into a hymn, the very one he was intoning at that moment, and each time my mother responded by breaking into tears of rage or pity, he beamed, delighted that mama, whose youth and beauty caused him to suspect her of impiety, owed him an act of contrition! How could fate have yoked two such dissimilar beings together? No matter how devout and mystical he was, my father was nevertheless a brute: in his eyes, were not my mother and I those units of wealth upon which Africans so prided themselves?

He had enrolled me in the school at the mission where he was employed; the priests accepted me in part at their own expense, probably to compensate in that way for the paltry salary they accorded him in return for a job that lasted until nightfall . . . . I was obliged to follow in their wake, crowned with the halo of my role as a choirboy who experienced an apothesis during Holy Week, when I lay down with my face to the floor next to the European celebrant, and especially when he washed me and kissed my feet . . . .

On that blessed day when I obtained the primary school diploma, my father, transfigured with joy, sang hymns until dawn. "It's the Holy Virgin who is responsible for your success! My prayer has been answered," he stammered. He rubbed his hands together, wept, and got up in the darkness to throw his arms around me. I stopped breathing and stiffened, unable to overcome the disgust that the smell of his dried sweat and early morning bad breath inspired in me; nevertheless, his tears moved me— they fell upon me as if sprinkled from an aspergillum. I in turn embraced him, but I immediately regretted it, my arms having turned to ice as they touched his hunchback. It made me furious to see him intruding into our joy; I had succeeded for my mother's sake, discharging a debt of secret happiness that I had contracted toward her in the hope that she might be able to forget her grief, if only for an instant, and that the wrinkle of bitterness, which had formed so prematurely on her still smooth face, might disappear . . . . I called to her. She ordered me to be quiet, but her voice was that of a happy woman.

Even now I can still feel the emotion I experienced that night. I waited impatiently for morning in order to see the happiness glistening in her eyes . . . .

Having obtained the primary school diploma at an age when people don't yet have hair between their legs, I was regarded as a prodigy; at that time the number of illiterates was so great in our part of the country that they flocked ceaselessly to our house, looking at me, touching me. I saw myself as a young civil servant—that was our ambition in those days— exempt from the whip of the *indigénat,** sporting an impressive pair of epaulets, and assured of a comfortable retirement. I loved life, and I was going to begin at a point where my elders had already reached their limits. This transport of happiness did not, alas, endure for long; my father, who skillfully surrounded himself with allies, had already decided upon my religious vocation. I yielded, not because a dozen old men came together for the express purpose of circumventing my plan and enjoined me from pursuing it, but because it seemed to me that, if the primary school diploma was the highest certificate available to the natives of my country, the seminary represented the forbidden paradise of Knowledge to which one could gain access with the Trojan horse of a religious vocation. My ruse was all that much easier to put into practice because Europeans, re- garding the matter scientifically, saw nothing more in the black man's penchant for entering orders than the simple manifestation of a religious temperament. Thus, I entered the minor seminary at T—— only to be expelled seven years later at the very moment when the timid stirrings of faith were, I believe, beginning to awaken in me. I had been compromised in an alleged affair of special friendship with a Gabonese mulatto, a puny but sensitive creature whom I pitied and took under my wing because his smell had made him the whipping boy of our class. He played the organ and introduced me to Handel, J.-S. Bach, and Mozart . . . . I would sit next to him and immediately fall into a pleasurable reverie as soon as his young girl's fingers settled upon the keyboard. His frailty, his smell, and the pride in his glance characterized for me his genius, which was, more- over, paradoxically vindicated in my eyes by his origins: he spoke not at all or very little about his mother, but it was for her sake, he confided in me, that he had decided to become a priest, and she was a young woman . . . .

We dreamed for hours on end about that musicians' Germany where our favorite composers had been born. Sometimes we became embroiled in discussions generated by the anxieties of faith; we felt a need to tran- scend ourselves in order to know each other, and in our skirmishes, I cheated, since I was the stronger, and obligingly allowed myself to be wounded in a harmless way. For me, Laurent was like a precocious

*A system of justice applied to the majority of Africans in the French colonial empire; it prescribed severe punishment for infractions like the failure to remove one's hat in the presence of a white administrator and was uniformly resented by African "sujets." Africans who became civil servants were elevated to the status of "évolués" and were no longer subject to the harsh jurisdiction of the *indigénat*. (tr)

younger brother; I encouraged his outbursts of enthusiasm and nurtured his genius. Yet, in spite of his sudden flashes of modesty, his abrupt revolts, and intense but ephemeral fits of obstinacy that could fool others, my passions succeeded little by little in absorbing him into me; he became my thing. That male propensity to protect him, to spare him from harmful idleness, hardly made me the pervert I may have seemed in the eyes of the priests. Now that I have gained some distance from the conflict that prostrated me in those days, now that life and the passage of years have freed me from it, I can say that even when I embraced Laurent, I by no means felt that sort of intoxication that desire breeds in me; I see it as a simple adolescent rapture, an unfortunate overflowing of the untamed vitality that had been suppressed in me by the austere life into which we were being initiated . . . . But the priests who had been observing us, spying on us, were of a quite different opinion; the expressions on their faces convinced me that any attempt to plead our case would be futile, that we were worse than dead for them. In my confused state of mind, I relived the affection I had felt for Laurent and examined it to detect some vague trace of the abnormal—in vain. My exuberance had tempered my friend's devotions, and it alone appeared to me capable of casting a venial blemish upon the tumultuous friendship that united us. I no longer knew what to think, alternately exculpating and blaming myself until, in the end, the very notion of sin lost all significance for me. The urge to believe encountered an implacable lucidity, and my expulsion from the seminary even accorded me a certain joy in the long run. It had been a decisive step for which my punctilious but passive nature had not taken the initiative; I found solace in that. At the thought of returning home, I was filled with the idealized image of my tender childhood, and it intensified in me the blissful urgency to cross the family threshhold once again. How can I conceal the sentiments that arose in me? Alas, I had placed too much faith in the joy my return was supposed to ignite. People had based exaggerated hopes on my success—wasn't I supposed to become the first black pope?—and my impromptu defection was regarded as a betrayal. The first person I encountered was my father, who refused to hear my side of the story and immediately took off his trousers as a means of cursing me; he ardently supported the strict observance of traditional rites and customs whenever they could serve to express his inherent vulgarity or spitefulness. After that I found myself relegated by general indifference to a tiny island of disdain. However, even then I couldn't find peace. I had thought that, by consummating the breach of our relationship, my fiasco would spare me the false compassion which Africans so deftly accord to those who fail and that I would not find myself under the obligation to relate the incident which had left me with a persistent malaise, but I was obliged to revise my expectations; wherever I went, importunate fools and indiscreet busybodies harpooned me with their useless questions, their embarrassing expressions of astonishment, or their vexatious commiseration. I came to resent them for it and even to hate them. All this sparked an indescribable nostalgia in me, heightened my fear of the future in a world where I seemed to be walking in my sleep, and exacerbated to the limit of credibility the vague regret which had taken the form of a vocation deferred. My rancor was piqued, and I began to imagine possibilities and means of gaining vengeance upon the director of the seminary. I spent entire days seeking to discover what might dislodge him for the rest of his declining years from his insufferable equanimity as a man absolutely certain of his Truth. Such thoughts preoccupied me, obsessed me. I surprised myself in the act of speaking when no one was there, repeating myself, rehearsing the seething remarks with which I would accost him. I became peculiar, eccentric; people got into the habit of speaking cautiously and circumspectly to me, or of remaining silent in my presence. And then there were rumors according to which my virtue, the alleged source of my torments, was unhinging my mind . . . . For women and men of a certain age, I suddenly became a specter. I quaked at the thought that they knew . . . oh, I hardly knew what I feared, but fear dwelt in me. My haughtiness having deceived certain inexpressible desires, people spread, at my expense, those monstrous lies upon which human rapacity nourishes itself . . . . As far as my father was concerned, he became convinced that the curses he had rained upon my head were taking effect in this form; he rejoiced and gave thanks to God in the conviction that a supernatural evil power was leagued against me, dispelling his apprehensions about once again daring to insult and humiliate my mother with impunity. Taking advantage of a heated argument to remove all such reservations from his mind, I began to look for work. I could have been hired by the largest employer in the country, the Administration, as a civil servant with title, but I had passed the age of appearances. Everything was highly centralized in the hands of the colonial authorities, and natives of the area were only recruited for carrying out orders that entailed no real responsibility. Such a politics of subservience would hardly enable me to realize myself. Thus, with an eye toward profit, I opted for the private sector. That is how I landed up with Monsieur Kriminopoulos, an old Cretan merchant . . . .

Two

Half asleep, my eyes burning, and with a cottony feeling in my mouth, I was already in the European section of town each morning by the first crowing of the cock, squatting on my haunches, ready to jump up at any moment and attack an invisible adversary with countless butts of the head, jabs, and kicks. Each store had its own solicitor, and together we gave battle to the cold as we waited, puffing and blowing on our fingers, for customers; in the pale half-light of the dawn, we positioned ourselves along the main business street in restless echelons of fantastic poles, mad lines of ghostly little telegraph poles. Each of us had a well-defined territory, hardly larger than the front of the store in which we happened to be employed, and once we had installed ourselves there, those revolting plots of coarse gravel, weeds, refuse, and animal excrement served as a red flag to pique our sense of honor and possessive instincts; for their sake we were prepared to lay down our lives, or those of our neighbors . . . .

Having himself arisen early, my boss, who appeared to have been carved from the same material as the mantle in the gas lamp that illuminated his figure, swallowed his greeting and pointed toward the street with an abrupt movement of his chin. I ran to take up my place there. It didn't take long for him to grow impatient behind the cash register against which his enormous crimson belly, intermittently visible between the ridiculous little striped flaps of his pyjama tops, would flatten itself at periodic intervals. When we heard the distant sounds of an approaching caravan of blacks from the bush, Monsieur Kriminopoulos, his turgid, veiny face studded with greenish pits, began to shout my name and to urge me on as if I were a dog. I took off my jacket, rolled up the bottoms of my trousers, verified the position of my glasses (which were constantly deserting my flattened nose), and charged, in the fog, into the invading mass of inky blackness that was constituted by a phalanx of simpletons who came to us by hamlets, villages, and half-starved tribes; they were frightened and

22

intent upon cashing in their harvests or their skeletal cattle and fleeing the town that weighed upon them and filled them with terror. Galvanized into action by the promise of a bonus and by the hysteria of our employers, we fought over this produce by deploying force or persuasion to divert animals and people into the shop, where an impulsive hubbub reigned amid filth, sweat, and the smells of palm oil, cocoa, and palmetto cabbages. I dove into this whirlwind of ragged women who were either pregnant or carrying a whiny brat in a sling across their backs, half-naked men, wheezing old geezers, and clamorous children; with my bloodshot eyes staring out of their sockets, I shouted, giving and receiving blows, falling down, and getting up again to hurl myself anew against those inhuman burdens of which I was taking possession, insensitive to the savageries of the porters who followed me until we were rolling at the feet of Monsieur Kriminopoulos, whose blue eyes suddenly reduced them to silence. When a thick, pink foam appeared at the tautened corners of my mouth and my legs trembled, I felt stabbing pains all over my body and could do no more than lie down on the crevice-filled cement of the veranda—I had lost my voice and sunk into a pleasurable gloom . . . . One afternoon, something happened to me almost without my being aware of it, and I caught myself succumbing to an opposite excess—an exaggerated and wholly unjustified optimism. Coming from a distance like an arrow that had missed some unknown target, a gratuitous happiness penetrated me and made me shudder; gone was that furtive sense of inexorable injustice which usually overcame me whenever I reflected seriously on my own situation. A strange excitement had taken hold of me; I wanted to hug my boss, play practical jokes, laugh. Perceiving the candy on the shelf, I experienced something like a fit of dizziness and lost all conception of the punishment I would incur. I knew that, as an accursed merchant, he would not tolerate people amusing themselves with such pranks in his shop. But the candy, like the forbidden fruit, fascinated me, and the risk I would be running merely heightened my excitement. I rose to the tips of my toes; suddenly, the candy ceased to attract me. I was more interested in creating a diversion that would oblige Monsieur Kriminopoulos to bolt from his slumber and surprise me with my hand in the candy jar, but the man, whose pimple-ridden skin was dripping with sweat, slept his lethargic sleep through all those broiling afternoons. Above and beyond his cataleptic repose, the Cretan demonstrated his disdain for me even better in a quite sonorous manner that was uniquely his own. As far as the object of my childish desire was concerned, it was forgotten in favor of the veranda and the mountain, shimmering above the icy glare of corrugated metal roofs and the inaudible drumming of undulant layers of heat; euphoric and with my jacket on my head, I chose that moment to leave Monsieur Kriminopoulos' shop forever and walk out into the African sun . . . .

I reached the market place, which was as sad and empty as the rest of the city. There I saw Yobla, in an execrable mood and with an old newspaper above his head. He was humming a tune just loud enough so that a preoccupied passerby could not ignore it, and it attracted my attention. He was sitting among a small group of counterfeit beggars who had come to compete unfairly against him with their sham infirmities. I underscored his authority by feverishly emptying my pockets into the chipped cup of his jagged fingers and hurrying away . . . . Behind the genuine leper, the *beignet*-sellers dozed in the shade of the awning on the slaughterhouse steps, their naked breasts erect like ears of corn and their skimpy loincloths, which were no more than thick strings around their waists, slipping across their legs. I had always felt a twinge of modesty when I looked in their direction during my visits to the market place. That concupiscent misery stilled my desire, disgusted me. Usually I hurried away from it, but this time I caught myself in the act of squinting toward the steps . . . .

Three

I didn't sleep that night and obliged my mother to listen to the endless chatter I inflicted upon her in my anguished, talkative mood. I did my utmost to vanquish the apathy with which she countered the exuberance of the role I was playing behind the mat that hung between our beds and served as a partition. I was convinced that luck had come my way in the person of a new employer, whom I could see talking to himself, his eyes glaring, in a living room covered with animal furs and inundated with the white light of a gas lamp hissing on an oblong stanchion that stood upright in the corner, between the refrigerator and the buffet, like a rude coffin of local manufacture . . . .

Seated on the couch, a glass of beer within reach, he was vociferating at the top of his voice. All at once, he bounded up like a wild beast on his short, stocky legs. His wife had just entered the room; her abbreviated neck was submerged between her thin shoulders, and her pointed shoulder blades, traversed at mid-point by the mauve hem of a low-cut dress, were quivering like a pair of enormous electric oyster shells . . . . Then came their daughter, timidly, a finger in her nose. She stood in front of the oblong stanchion, her head bowed, her legs slightly apart, and I shuddered to see her outlined against the backdrop of that lugubrious piece of furniture. Suddenly, the thunderous explosion of her father's voice was followed by a confused tinkling on the cement floor where shards of glass were falling from the window pane against which Monsieur Gruchet had hurled his beer-glass, and the little wench was flinging herself against her mother's thighs and beginning to bang her head in desperation against the older woman's groin, while tentacular spurts of blood slithered all around the child's "already" promising legs, glistened like a tangled skein of crazy silk threads in the white light of the lamp; they were oozing from her flared skirt, turning liquid, and forming frothy whirlpools beneath the door . . . .

"Look at that!" shouted the father. "Only ten years old!"

25

"Eight!" mewed the mother, but he didn't hear her any more than he had seen her, because he was now shouting and cursing not his wife or daughter, whose age he didn't even know, but that absent, unidentified individual to whom he referred with exclamations of ". . . those people! Them! Gee! Haw . . . ," hysterical and unintelligible little groans, frenzied gestures and mockeries—it made him foam at the mouth—and whom in the end he characterized as a wretched priest, a red-necked Dutch peasant.

"Isn't that right, my friend?"

I merely dropped my nose and offered him a view of the kinky hair on my head: the affairs of white men had nothing to do with me. I simply wanted them to help me, because they by themselves owned the largest share of the world's wealth . . . . It had all been very unexpected. Instead of howling out his demands for women to sleep with Europeans, as he had been doing for the past twenty years in the manner of an itinerant auctioneer, the white-haired houseboy, whose controlled, pliant voice followed upon the miserable metallic clanking of the cracked bell in the black part of town, had been calling to me . . . .

After we had walked for a while in silence, absorbed in our attempt to survive the ceaseless volleys of nocturnal insects—the cold, winged molecules from the gloom that crackled in our faces—the houseboy stopped to tell me: "It good ting you been deh, eben when you done what fo' dey sen' you 'way. You lea'n many, many, many ting, and you been some 'un, eben when it be me, a pooh basta'd flunky fom Loango, who done say so . . . . Don' was' time like dat, like you got some 'un who done die in de dese't a Libya where dey fit deh wa'. Do some ting like what I been sayin to ma sef, boy: people cain't lib if'n dey no got wo'k, on'y boozin' and makin lob an' profinatin' de Good Lawd. I'se satisfied like I is, what ebe' he done ta me. Sho he would'a whallop me, if'n I had'n foun' yuh. Sho ting . . . an' deh he is so full wid booze dat he done take it in his haid to wa'k on watah like de Lawd . . . ."

He blew his nose loudly.

"Eben when people did'n get no ting out'a it, dey could'n ta had no fun'al if he wa'nt some un who hab de idea ta put hiz pants in de coffin a' wid a bottle he been d'inkin so as ta seem jus' like. Ain't it sad to en' up like dat? Well den, if'n he'd a listen'd ta me, if'n he'd a gone ta school, would'n it a been him who had got de job what no niggah basta'd in dis count'y ebe' got befo' and what is now going ta yuh—lea'nin book to Madamoiselle?"

" . . . ."

"Oh, it did'n happ'n jus' like dat. When de whi' man need some un who ain't white, it's cuz tings ain't going so well wid his bruthahs. We done laugh ou' sef silly. 'Gid de hell out'a hea,' he say to de uddah un. 'Scoun'l, sex pe've't,' he ansh back as he run ta hiz ca'. He goin ta fall down, I sez ta my sef, cuz hiz haid stickin so fa' out as he run to de ca' doah, dat he done leab open like by acciden'. An' eben when he inside, he done stick hiz bea'd out da winnow a bit ta yell, 'sex pe've't' at Massah who run out ta plan' one on him. 'Wait! What he done, Zacques,' shout de Madame. 'Ol' monkey!' Massah yell back ta he'; dats de en', I sez ta my sef. Dey goin ta kill one anuddah. De uddah un don' go, but he hab hiz clodhoppah nex ta de gaz like by acciden'. He make one big ba'rummm, when Massah get deh ta plan' a good un on him, an' den he take off so fas' he sen' Massah up in de ai' like a ai'plane wid de back a hiz ca'. He goin so fas' I tells my sef de Holy Ghos' jus' lef dat place . . . ."

"But to . . . ."

"He hab a nice, nice way a singin de mass. Eben I unne'stan dat ri' 'way wehn I been gone to mass like by acciden'. Eben I unne'stan why Massah lef' behin' hiz newspapehs, hiz books, his whiskey, an' his niggah ladies f'om de black pa't a town ta go ta mass on Sundays. Eben when Madame tink he' husban' no longah got de eye fo' any but dem niggah ladies, he done come back ta de st'aight an' na'ow. Ah, de ol' who'! Ain't me dat sez wheh he hid dem niggah ladies what sings de mass so good. Sho ain't me dat tells de Lawd 'bout it . . . ."

"Ahah! So that's the reason . . . you mean to say . . . in the end . . . it was that priest who was giving lessons to Mademoiselle? How old can she be?"

"Yessuh. He say he be lookin fo' some un who done lea'n someting fo' ta teach hiz daughtah. 'Is you all idiots?' he as' me. He done hab 'nuff a whi' mens. Den I been real glad ta tell him I knows yuh, how as yuh spen' all dat time ta become Massah Faddah befo' de p'iests done kick yuh out a deh cuz you some un . . . ."

"Let's not exaggerate, and what about Madame?"

"Oh! She no coun' fo' no ting. Dey ain't no one who's goin ta heaben like Madame just to go deh . . . !"

A sudden change took place inside me; I was on the verge of turning back. But why should such an affair make any difference to me? I had to earn my living . . . . I touted my new job by citing figures; my mother, who had been sorely deceived in her expectations of life, retained a firm grip on reality, so materialistic that she might well have passed for a niggardly old woman. But that night my visions of a brilliant future *à la* Rockefeller were all in vain; under these circumstances, her silent presence on the other side of the mat became even more distressing, and had it not been for the barely audible clinking of the bracelets she seemed to be cursing, I would have thought she was dead. As her sibylline reserve became increasingly intolerable, I multiplied my figures, appropriating for myself the monied world for which we had the morbid obsession of all poor people. Sometimes I paused to catch my breath, listening intently to detect a glimmer of cheefulness on the other side of the mat. But there was nothing, nothing at all. I imagined her lying on her back, exhausted, her eyes open in the half-light, and I experienced an almost irresistable urge to cry, for one would have thought that she had ceased to live or that she had evanesced into one of those tangles of darkness scattered through the yellowish haze engendered by a misbegotten, early-morning sun and was now expiring through the tiny cracks in the mud walls . . . . She could not help but laugh, at least inwardly, about my garrulousness, and she restrained herself to avoid giving me the pleasure of hearing the voice that had once sufficed to make me happy, in the olden days when we could unconstrainedly give ourselves over to the tender and innocent games of mother and child; perhaps it was those memories that caused me to prattle on as if I were drunk, or perhaps it was the obstinacy of my desire to discover some compelling reason that might shatter her indifference: although it no longer happened very often, she used to laugh a good deal in those days, at the time when I would cunningly lift my arm and grab her neck before slipping around behind her, as she vigorously defended herself with the twin barrier of her adjoined hands and, her eyes closed, burst into a laugh that was as cool as the water on the vines in the forest and that, as an eruption of the health and exuberance she usually concealed beneath the old man's tyrannical regime, had the capacity to dissipate her fits of anger; we would abandon her ramshackle hut to run into the high grass left by the last rainy season, to gambol through the shallow surrounding forest where papayas and guavas—the succulent missiles of our playful frolics—grew in abundance, and to return home only after the ominous, cruciform shadow of a nocturnal toucan had glided over our heads. A lack of money had, alas, deprived me of that joy . . . . In desperation, I began to fantasize aloud about a universe where whirlwinds of francs cavorted and forests of bills from the Bank of French Equatorial Africa rippled in the breeze;* in the end, by virtue of nourishing myself on these pecuniary chimeras, a miracle occurred, for I caught myself sporting the self-satisfied sneer of the successful nigger who has nothing to worry about for the rest of his life . . . . My mother burst into sobs. "My poor child, how you can play such a despicable role in front of us!" She continued to cry more energetically than ever and quite noisily at first, as her curled-up body rolled from one side of the bed to the other, making the bamboo slats creak and grazing the raffia mat, which ballooned out when she came in contact with it only to recede and balloon out again as she moved in the opposite direction and immediately returned . . . . At

*In francophone Africa, the franc C.F.A. is issued by the Bank of French West Africa and the Bank of French Equatorial Africa. Tied to the French currency system, it is worth one-fiftieth of a French franc. (tr)

such times my father suddenly experienced the call of nature and left to study the plants at the back of the house while awaiting the silent phase of these crises, which always provoked in me a tenderness tinged with fear; had I tried to console her then, I would have been met with a rebuff; I knew the spirited temperament of my mother, whose moments of weakness could easily turn into fits of rage, and for that reason I waited until I heard the intermittent gasps in which her dying force spent itself before I went over and sat down on the edge of her bed, which still shook under the influence of her heavy breathing.

"That woman!" she cried in a voice quivering with impotent rage.

We withdrew into a moment of mutual silence: she profoundly agitated and worrying about how to cure me of the madness that her unerring and perpetually suspicious maternal instinct had feared—the love of a white woman, the sort of thing that, according to her, overstepped the bounds of reason and threatened to be the ruin of her son—and me equally furious at her brutal approach to the issue and my own incapacity to conceal my emotions, seeking some artifice, a whole mountain of artifice, that might neutralize her prescient indiscretion.

"Mad! Stark raving mad!" she muttered to herself. "Women! But choose one from the neighborhood! What good does it do to complicate life even more . . . . A white woman! Do you have the slightest notion? And married on top of it all! And you know . . . her husband . . . is one of those white men who would take a potshot at you for a trifle . . . ."

"Mama . . . ."

"Oh!" she exclaimed in a broken voice, "I'm doing my duty . . . . I've never warned you . . . ."

"Mama!" I replied, "you're imagining things!" My anger prevented me from continuing, and I collapsed on my mother's shoulder, that childhood pillow which cradled my frail neck and which, unchanged after so many years, I always rediscovered with a bitter, melancholy joy, as if nothing had changed since then, as if I were still a baby wailing on the pile of old clothes she had placed under my back to soften my repose on the barren bamboo bed where I had seen the light of day and where the dawn, filtered through the cracks in the wall, now found us positioned as time had frozen us, as if, abandoned by everyone, we had eluded the passage of years with the crystallized sense of pity we felt for ourselves. That was no longer the place where I wanted to be, for I seemed to be participating in my own beginnings, as if Aki Barnabas was going to be conceived anew and ejected from maternal bowels unto this wretched bed that had, until now, been the only stable reference point in my life. Then, in my desire to suffer and to revivify myself with the blood from her old wounds, which had been reopened by the memories I insisted upon keeping alive, I grasped my mother tightly in my arms . . . . She was not fooled and lavished on me none of those resounding kisses that she habitually planted on my forehead under such circumstances, nor any of those words that had the capacity to transfigure the world for me when they issued from her mouth; she remained stiff and cold next to me, as if she were intent upon listening to the throbbing of a heart that I too felt beating in the shoulder upon which my cheek was resting. I recognized it as one of her rebellions without sighs or tears, one of those anguished spells that I dreaded, and I was on the verge of breaking the silence, of taking all the blame upon myself; at that instant I sensed my mother distancing herself from me, abandoning me. "Mama!" I cried and immediately felt ashamed of myself. I felt an uncontrollable urge to play my ace in the hole, to outdo myself, to confound her; the occasion appeared to me opportune for a clarification: I had become a man, and my mother didn't seem to care, although at my age people in our neighborhood were already heads of households and even polygamists. "Aha! Yes, indeed," I thought, "I didn't realize how to react in time; I'll have to assure her that she will always be my mother, the only woman one can ever love without resentment, the only woman one never forgets!" I moved away from her shoulder. She stared intently at me, like a madwoman: it was growing later in the morning, and I could see the large pupils of her eyes; they were so dilated that they seemed to have been stricken by sclerosis, and they gleamed intermittently with the phosphorescent lustre of a luminous glass; her gaze sometimes fell upon me but immediately wandered in another direction—maybe she was seeing little Barnabas in his short pants, the only Barnabas who was still a son to her, or maybe she was already mourning my corpse, riddled with Monsieur Gruchet's volleys of buckshot. Two halting tears rolled across her cheeks. I was annoyed by the situation.

"Mama!" I interjected in a harsh tone of voice.

She took my face in her hands, flung back the upper part of her body, and leaned her shoulders against the wall. Then her timid hands moved hesitantly up across my face, which she began to caress and palpitate as if she wanted to engrave its rough spots onto her calloused palms; her fingers glided over my eyebrows, the sides of my nose, the edges of my lips, the protuberances of my jawbones. She drew me toward her and finally graced my forehead with a kiss.

"Poor Barnabas!" she moaned, and her lament pierced me like a poison dart.

Four

In the place of the virgin forest, our African forest, that primeval frenzy of grass, vines, and all those natural essences that rushed away in delirious waves, jostling each other and forming a saw-tooth silhouette on the horizon, they had substituted an elegant but anemic little French formal garden, from which the birds seemed to hold themselves aloof . . . . Here and there a few weeping willows, prostrated by the heat, sulked in their solitude and bowed their scorched brown heads in disheveled despair *vis-à-vis* the indifference of the stiff, proud, imperturbable pine trees which endured their exile with dignity and a serenity that they cast, like their shadows, across the pathways. Elsewhere, natives wearing white smocks and armed with sprinkling cans bustled about mumbling a sinister chant among the clumps of roses, gladioli, tulips, carnations, and chrysanthemums that they were arranging in hotbeds like terminally ill patients in hibernation, while the scarlet blooming of an enormous poinciana rustled above a brightly-colored villa that could be seen at the tapered peak of a pathway lined with phormiums.

Completely absorbed in her own thoughts, Madame Gruchet received me with a start, uttered a faint cry, and turned pale. I felt a gust of ether running through my bones and freezing the marrow; I dared not turn around—it was as if some unidentified danger were lurking at my heels and I suddenly became of aware of its furtive presence as a result of the woman-of-the-house's muffled cry, which resounded like an echo from the other side of an abyss where she was shouting a warning to me! Sometimes no more than a trifle sufficed to inspire me in those senseless fears that overcame me at certain times and that are even now cowering in my adult soul like fireflies in the sunlight—fears that, as my mother used to say, made me scream in terror when I was small. I would have remained in the doorway, if Madame Gruchet, recovering her wits, had not brusquely motioned me toward an armchair. Fortunately, the woman, who then ex-

31

perienced something like a fit of obliviousness, no longer paid any attention to me, having begun to pace up and down the living room; otherwise, upon seeing me so nervous, she might have lectured me like a servant, and I was apprehensive about being treated in that way, perhaps because I had completed the first part of my *baccalauréat* or perhaps because I was the only native in town to wear gold-rimmed glasses, a Christmas present from a saintly Breton woman, whose Christian charity, or an exotic but impersonal love of her neighbor, had transformed the near-sighted little seminarian that I was at the time into her well-pleased beneficiary . . . .

. . . Inscrutable, Madame Gruchet passed back and forth in front of me, sometimes even brushing against me with the pleats of her dress, which emanated a perfume that left me with an aftertaste of honey on my tongue. She circled the single old Chippendale table, walked over toward the casement window through which several flowering branches of the enormous poinciana that rustled upon the roof could be seen swaying just above the ground, twirled about and, like a caged animal, recommenced her restless pacing . . . .

Returning for a second time from the window, she finally flopped down on a chair in front of me. Like a compass needle caught in my magnetic field, she fixed her dull gaze upon me, and my response was limited to an occasional involuntary tremor that resembled a reflex action. Like two deaf mutes unaware of each other's presence, we remained in this position for minutes that seemed like centuries to me. A number of times I was on the verge of breaking the silence to address the problem that seemed to be preoccupying her: maybe she was thinking that her husband had bestowed the honor of his preferment upon me as a reward for some revolting service I had performed for him during his life of debauchery. I knew him by sight and by reputation. People said he had salted and canned all his pigs when the Second World War was declared. I only remembered his large glasses; he suffered from a strange eye disease that, by virtue of a no less strange coincidence, made its appearance at the outbreak of hostilities and disappeared completely when they ceased. Nevertheless, he had modified his wardrobe, draping himself with khaki and sporting two strips of gold braid on his epaulettes. On my way to school, I had been able to catch glimpses of him, his helmet covered with grass and banana leaves and a gun in his hands as he played war with the newly recruited natives in the drainage ditches of the town, although his troops were far too solemn to execute their maneuvers with a show of good will. And when the troops left for the North, he did not go with them, but rather came to live out his fantasies of love with a remarkably well-endowed negress in the native section of the town. In the end, he disappeared. People thought that a miracle had occurred, but it didn't take them long to begin singing a different tune when they descried him next to another buxom negress in a magnificent Primaquatre that, in lieu of a hood orna- ment, flaunted a French flag with the Cross of Lorraine emblazoned across the middle of its white stripe. People lost themselves in conjecture: some thought the war was over, but a few ill-famed negresses, who were extremely well-informed about current events, soon set them straight; others then assumed he had simply gone to Yaoundé and even to Chad but was sent back to Ngaoundéré with a fever after rumors began to cir- culate about a bomb having fallen on Fort-Lamy; finally, one of his cur- rent black mistresses related that he had succeeded in having himself dis- charged for medical reasons. . . . And since then, he acquired the habit of trotting on horseback through the black neighborhood, where his café-au- lait bastards and his silk pyjamas, hung out to dry, could be seen just about everywhere . . . .

. . . I was yearning to assure his wife that my preferment had come about by pure accident and that I would gladly forego it, if doing so could be of any solace to her. But as often happens, the angriest people are those who are pitied the most. Did she read something from the uncon- scious movement of my lips? Madame Gruchet jumped up as if she had been bitten by a tarantula and regarded me with scorn from the height of her standing position. Some sort of transformation seemed to have taken place in her: the blood that rose to her temples gave new life to her emaci- ated waxen face, the traits of which were being gradually effaced by the pitiless African sun, and made her look younger, more beautiful. My im- portunate vanity was gratified, even flattered; wasn't I the cause of her uneasiness, her exasperation, her sudden transformation? "Love," I thought, "sometimes appears under the guise of hatred, and a woman can actually love someone she does not respect . . . . She betrayed herself, for like me she feels the affinity, or fatality, that links unwitting protagonists in an unavoidable rendezvous with destiny . . . ." Tears came to my eyes . . . . I would have stopped there, if she had had the spunk to throw me out, but my idea of the white woman's freedom to make her own decisions was a bit too abstract; a petty bourgeois woman who had certainly been a virgin on her wedding day, the pious Madame Gruchet was no doubt mesmer- ized by the sacrosanct authority of husbands and could hardly indulge herself in crossing a lord and master who had hired me without consulting her.

"And . . . and as Monsieur told you yesterday," she said in a harsh tone of voice, "you will start at nine o'clock in the morning after I return from mass; I will draw up your schedule . . . . You will not have much difficulty with my daughter, if you know how to go about it, for she is an intelligent, quick-witted child . . . ."

"She would never dare," I went on thinking; "she is as silent as a carp

and would always know how to keep a secret; and because she is absolutely convinced of her invulnerability behind the shield of a fidelity in
which she steeped herself until she has become fully impregnated with it,
she would not even admit she had been violated . . . . And yet I sense her
distress, surmise the questions which she is asking herself about me and
which culminated in the panegyric she just delivered to me on the subject
of her daughter . . . ."

"I do not think you will be able to live on the premises; we already
have a great deal of difficulty providing lodging for our . . . ."

"I am not a servant, madame. I have a home and a mother to support,"
I interrupted, vexed at having to play the role of a dutiful child.

She had regained her self-assurance in speaking to me as if I were one
of her houseboys, but the mischievous smile that crossed my bulbous lips
immediately caused her to abandon her haughty demeanor and gave rise
to a sudden shiver . . . . I began to ask myself if we were alone, if the time
when everything was still possible might not be running out, if I shouldn't
try my luck like a Hussar so that Madame Gruchet, assaulted in this manner, might voluntarily give herself to me or promise to give herself to me,
when she suddenly arose on the pretext of going to look for her daughter,
who had been listening to us all the while, staring at us through the keyhole of the first door to the left of the corridor leading from the veranda to
the back yard, the door behind which the little girl's shriek echoed and at
once died away descrescendo to the noisy and chaotic accompaniment of
her hurried footsteps as she ran away from the other side of the partition. I
felt relief from my moment of excitement verging on panic. But gradually
her pretext began to seem like an escape, a coquette's invitation, an
expression of her need to reassure me, to guide my steps, to beguile me
onto the forbidden ground where she desired to entice me, a mischievous
expedient on the part of a woman in love . . . . I felt as if I had grown up in
a single instant, attaining a sense of completeness which momentarily
endowed me with the retrospective conviction that something had been
lacking—an undefinable something that had been lost in the night of time
and had just been unexpectedly returned to me. I marvelled at myself, a
legless cripple who had been miraculously healed and was alternately
dumbfounded and overjoyed to touch, to caress, to rejoice over the legs
that had grown back during sleep. One could well have said that until then
the universe had been sinking into the dust with me and that we had just
risen, drawing ourselves up with a single movement. Like roiling water
pent behind a dam, my prospects burst forth in gigantic fantails of spray
that clove the heavens of ambition; Madame Gruchet would ask for a
divorce, and her husband would be unable to prevent her from being
happy, even though he might be Mephistopheles and Falstaff all rolled
into one; nothing stops a woman in search of her own happiness, and

there is no court in which one can plead against the reasons of the heart. Monsieur Gruchet would avoid a scandal by helping us leave Cameroon. Everyone knew he was capable of anticipating his own widowerhood by sending his wife back to spend her final days in Europe. "He couldn't help but take advantage of this unexpected windfall," they would say. "She disgusts him, with her pretentions of fidelity!" As for me, he would spare me for the sake of someone he could no longer love, and the two of us would embark for France! I had never laid eyes upon that country, but I had been taught since earliest childhood to sing the praises of its genius and beauty; indeed, I felt so much affinity for it that I asked myself if I hadn't been a Frenchman in some previous incarnation . . . .

Yet nothing had actually taken place between this woman and myself to justify such hopes. I had allowed myself to be so taken in by her show of emotion that I prided myself upon having an intuitive understanding of her soul. But despite the burning temptation to savor my triumph, my happiness, the thought of making bold, taking matters into my own hands, and inducing her to corroborate my intimations by acknowledging her love filled me with a sense of shame, an embarrassing timidity; never could I have feared Madame Gruchet as much as I did in loving her. I preferred the invisible bonds of secrecy and silence, while at the same time relinquishing any contrary initiative to that languid woman, who, swallowing the disappointments of marriage, had devoted herself entirely to God. Naively I compared her to a stick of dynamite being slowly consumed by its own fire as onlookers despair of ever seeing it explode. She fascinated me, titillated me with all the romantic associations of the forbidden white woman, and my restless, excitable, passionate nature had transformed this sentiment into something which transcended all bounds as I repeatedly fashioned it anew in the forge of my desire, imagining in her an ardor that was exaggerated by my own African sensuality. I could only visualize her in a constant state of disarray, flushed and beaded with perspiration in the blissful deep sleep of love. All this was oscillating back and forth in my head and wearing me out. I became particularly conscious of it while on the veranda facing the high hill (the veranda of her villa, that is): she had had a desk installed there for her daughter and for me a bare table with a chair—my office. It was there that I lived without seeing her, since all the tasks which occupied Madame Gruchet were invariably performed, with the military precision of a conscientious housekeeper, at the same times and in the same parts of the house. And while the shameless daughter bent over her desk and played with herself (the swaying of her little body toward the right, her pellucid complexion, and her vacant stare gave her away), I could follow the mother through the various rooms to which her duties took her by listening to the sound of her sandals, which plop-plopped all day long in my head, where the unbending Madame

Gruchet was constantly trampling upon my ideas. My thoughts could no longer stray from her, whether she was eating breakfast, writing a letter, composing a bouquet of flowers to the sound of pruning shears, taking a shower, or even flushing the toilet. I lived only for that woman, whose arid body had been unable to hold the interest of a husband smitten with the charms of buxom Negresses, and at times, incapable of waiting until the next day to see her again, I abandoned the native section of town to reconnoiter as far as the cast-iron gate of her villa. There, haunted by the fear of being discovered, I experienced every sort of anguish; reacting as if by reflex, my Adam's apple danced feverishly in a neck stretched toward the illuminated translucent casement window, behind which the shadows of the Gruchet family glided about; I stood there waiting for I don't know what until all the lights went out and darkness engulfed the house, a veil of inconsolable sorrow.

My mother would have continued to close her eyes, acting as if nothing had happened or as if nothing had changed between us, if I had not begun to drink. Unfortunately for her, I was an effusive drunkard, alternately sad and joyful like all neophytes unaccustomed to the effects of alcohol, and from time to time I came to weep or laugh derisively on her shoulder, which shook with indignation. She began to avoid me. In vain she left the house as soon as I awoke to spare me an inevitable daily embarrassment, for I was drunk almost every evening; I sensed that she was preoccupied and bitter. But the ways of the Lord are many; it was under the influence of alcohol that I came close to finding Him for the first time: one day when I was so drunk I thought myself in heaven, I sent a sizeable money order to the Reverend Father D—— with the request that he say a high mass for me.

Five

It was the beginning of the rainy season, which would last for two or three months—a time for whiskey, firesides, tales and legends . . . .

On my way to mass, I once again found myself in that bleak landscape overhung with a belly of clouds and smoking as if some noisome volcano had been turned upside down on the flooded earth, where a frothy sheet of water was about to prance fiendishly across everything, collapsing graves and transforming corpses into nomads as if they were of no more value than the corks, empty bottles, rusty slop-pails, banana peels, and all the other refuse, debris of all kinds, that was now going to accompany them on their journey, surrounding them with symbolically ironic swatches of old tinsel that had been ripped from its place of honor as a makeshift way of honoring their anticipated resurrection . . . .

I continued my way in a succession of brief pauses to shield my face momentarily from the blasts of a metallic wind that whistled like a spitting viper. From time to time, my reflection emerged from an adjacent pool and bounded like a jungle cat toward my neck. How could I believe that this brachycephalic head was mine—this head on which the handful of hair thrown at it by some Practical-Joker-God seemed not to have taken, this head into which the temples and cheeks had sunk as if someone had pulled them from the inside and refused to let go, this head whose haggard, dirty eyes glowed with an evil flame as if they were the only openings into hell . . . ? Once again I found myself in the little church, which was so somber that I thought at first glance it was hung in black. "A requiem!" I reflected, annoyed and distressed as I walked up the central aisle. I would have gone as far as the first row of pews if I hadn't recognized my father's hunchback (my eyes had become accustomed to the gloom)— the hunchback that symbolized his misery and was now threatening to burst through his pretentious beadle's uniform. Kneeling all alone in plain view near the communion table, he was more picturesque than ever—

motionless in one of his ludicrous meditations, cradling his face in one hand and supporting himself with the other on a rude halberd of local fabrication on the very spot, not far from the tabernacle, where a luminous halo fell from the chandelier. My mother and I had not been aware of his new promotion. His uniform was black with silver braid and a matching two-pointed military student's hat, all in all rather solemn and sinister, but papa was barefoot, and the effect was not what it might have been; the man who begat me seemed like a distracted academician, who, upon jumping out of bed, had just slipped on his formal jacket. The surprise and burst of laughter that I had suppressed caused me to perform my genuflection the wrong way, like a drunken catechist, before beating my retreat into the crowd to escape detection. I dared not let my father see me: either he would die of shock, or he would make straight for me and deliver a public sermon. Fortunately, the little cathedral was as dark as a cave, and my father, an old black fellow whose eyesight was failing, remained utterly oblivious in his tunnel-like gloom. The silhouette of Brother Hégésippe, whose gelatinous posterior brushed against his cassock and streaked it with moisture, outlined itself pleasantly in my mind; he was a brilliant architect whose only teacher had been the "open book of nature." His church was the mirror image of our forests, everything on the vertical, a bit tortuous, densely packed, filled with tension . . . . A few small windows twinkled in the false night of the arched vault at the level of two large, pretentious towers that extended fervently skyward like giant microphones seeking to capture the word of God. Scattered over the cool paving tiles, the natives were as completely happy there as if they had found themselves in the calm shade of a thicket into which the sun never penetrated.

The mass had not yet started when I arrived. The faithful were praying, and the drone of mumbled prayers arose from their hypnotized assemblage, a macabre litany accompanied by the drumming of raindrops on the cement tiles. The scene was so dismal that I no longer knew if the icy grip on the back of my neck and around my ankles was the effect of the cold or a premonition of death. I closed my eyes.

Upon reopening them, I saw my father still prostrating himself next to the holy table at the very spot where I myself had kneeled to take my first communion eight years earlier in the midst of young girls all dressed in white. I had expected a great deal from that solemn moment, hoping that my eyes would finally be opened to the majestic light of Christ, that I-don't-know-what would be revealed to me, convincing me that the Lord could indeed be identified with those wafers which I knew had been prepared by an illiterate, syphilitic baker, whose voice was heard every night in the black section of town as that of the muezzin calling for his faithless pig. In vain I stared at the crucifix, the plaster Virgin, and the other images;

nothing came alive, nothing moved, even after the manducation of the eucharist. I had even questioned the girl next to me about the apparent transformation that had overtaken her, for she was crying and sniffling so much that, exasperated by a ceremony which seemed to last forever, my yearning turned to nausea. Her only response was to stick out her tongue unobtrusively at me as she devoted herself to a snotty-nosed purring interspersed with occasional moans; other young girls and then several boys began to imitate her, perhaps fooling themselves as well as the electrified audience into believing that we had actually just seen the Lord! Despite my urge to vomit, which I had acknowledged upon leaving the church, and my repeated denials, my father spent months asking me whether or not I too had seen Him. "Why would anyone be ashamed of that?" he asked me angrily each time and boxed my ears, forcing me to kneel and pray with him, as if he were obliging me to do penance for having told a lie.

Who could have guessed that several months later we would be setting down his coffin at this same site—a coffin that had been rough-hewn by a crafty and cantankerous carpenter who had just lost his wife and his virility in a automobile accident, a coffin that would momentarily unite me with some anonymous chap who, in a fit of Christian charity, had offered the top of his head to lighten the burden on my own, for we ourselves sometimes take the place of a hearse in this country without funeral parlors; our heads on fire, we staggered through the mud that was slimy and alive in the rainy season when each drop of water seems to beget a worm—they come in all sizes and colors: pink, purple, and violet earthworms, bicephalic worms, tricephalic worms with heads of asps, vipers, and tapeworms, a rainy-season annelid world that could in a few days transform a dead elephant into a skeleton so immaculate it would deserve to be put on display in a museum, and we were going to inter my father in this voracious mud as we struggled along behind the reverend father D——, who had rolled up the bottom of his cassock and was goose-stepping to his off-key rendition of "Miserere mei Deus," while my father's emaciated body rolled above my head and clumped ceaselessly about like a mole carrying a heavy load and stumbling across an attic floor; he was constantly off balance due to the hunchback that, undiminished by death, caused him to bump the thin planks of the coffin with a lugubrious frequency, as if his body were swaying to the rhythm of an invisible metronome that was nothing other than our waddling through the viscid mud into which my mother passionately threw herself (although she didn't stay there), for she had perhaps instinctively sensed the impending and sudden end several weeks earlier when she had regained her husband's domicile as the result of an altercation we had had one evening after I returned home drunk at an extremely late hour. "It's all my fault . . . . All

we needed was that white woman to . . . ." I thought she was going to col-
lapse under the efforts she was making to lift the bulging old suitcase that
anchored her to the ground, despite desperate yanks with her entire body
as her incisors clamped down on her in-drawn lower lip and her long, frail
arms became stretched taut by the weight of the burden.

Her departure had staggered me, thrust me into a state of hostility and
anger. But I was calmed by the thought that she was unhappy beneath her
peevishness, and I even went so far as to despise my need for freedom, a
pet idea that impelled me to dream hypocritically about ways of putting
an end to our life together. I fell into a panic at the notion that my mother
might foresake me in spite of my subsequent apologies, abandoning me
to the fathomless solitude that lurked over me in the middle of the night;
even the distant prospect of living with another woman had always frightened me to the extent that I avoided love affairs, those seeds of a habit
that would have found extremely favorable soil in my phlegmatic temperament; my mother had spoiled me so completely that I was more suited to
relish the comforts of such company than to share its responsibilities. I felt
humiliated by the fact that she was leaving me just as she had left my
father, and I grew indignant at the thought of having come to resemble
him in any way . . . . Lurching unsteadily as if under the influence of a
heavy sea, she somehow managed to raise the suitcase to her thigh at first
and then onto her left shoulder; as her body bent into a painful stoop, she
positioned it slantwise across the base of her neck; with her head resting
upon her other shoulder and her shadow, like that of an overburdened
Atlas, spreading out toward a doorway drenched in moonlight, she left
hurriedly, ponderously, like a stevedore rushing his bulky load toward the
gangplank after having been galvanized into action by the shriek of the
ship's sirens during the confused hubbub of departure.

With a start, I leaped after her, almost knocking her from the veranda,
where she seemed to be awaiting this final outburst.

"I'll be glad to wait until morning," she said, "but I'm not unpacking my
things . . . ."

She smiled sadly, staring straight ahead, preoccupied; the flickering
flame of the hearth danced in her tear-filled eyes.

"Nawoma,"* I cried as I collapsed on her shoulder.

She did not push me away, but rather hugged me fervently, whispering,
"I would like this night to be like the old days when I piled my old rags
under your back to make your bed softer and when I slid my arm beneath
your head to serve as a pillow . . . . I was happy then . . . . What has
happened to you?"

I was so much in need of consolation and forgiveness that I pressed

---

*"Mama" in the Beti language of South-Central Cameroon.

myself passionately against her and promptly fell asleep. She took advantage of the situation to leave quietly . . . .

We were not to meet again until the funeral of my father, whose corpse had been discovered after a storm in a vegetable patch of the kitchen-garden at the mission; his lips, gums, and eyes had been half eaten by ants and worms . . . . Then there was the burial in the rain; we experienced so much difficulty lowering the coffin into the rain-filled grave that we finally felt obliged to weight it with stones; it took a nose-dive into the open pit, sending up a jet of muddy water that hit me like a slap in the face while the reverend father D——, who had rolled his hassock up to his belt and whose large wet beard was no more than a sort of yellowish tail swinging back and forth beneath his lower lip, hastened toward the comforting toddy that was no doubt waiting for him . . . .

My mass had not yet begun; an asthmatic old organ intoned the nasal prelude of an introit, and I scrutinized the organist, his fingers, which in every respect resembled those of lascivious old men whose bald heads shine at the feet of naked dancers in the first row of a burlesque theater, grew weaker in proportion to the flickering of the candles. I knelt, mechanically made the sign of the cross, and, finding I had nothing to say to Him, sat down while beginning to observe my father. I could recognize him by the luminescence of his braid and the silhouette of his beadle's uniform; still kneeling next to the communion table, he finally arose and traversed the nave in ghostly silence as his bare feet slid across the tiles of the central aisle that we in turn would later be obliged to descend to the singing of the *Dies irae* and burdened with his coffin, which caused us to veer from right to left, from left to right. How could I have known that my father was mimicking his own funeral procession for me, only pausing from time to time at the very spots where we would briefly catch our breath so as not to fall too far behind the reverend father D——, who had already passed through the church portal and was himself trotting awkwardly behind his choirboys because he was having difficulty keeping his cassock out of the mud.

And my father was coming closer; the little excrescence of flesh that was crushing his neck became more and more luminous, more and more fantastic, when conjoined with the glitter of his braid. He stopped at the level of my pew and then moved away to continue his route down that central aisle which seemed like the guiding principle of his miserable life and along which he had plodded submissively with the resignation of an old draught ox until he enjoyed a monopoly on the right to walk there and the surface itself gleamed like the arm of a river stagnating in the shade . . . . Suddenly, the melancholy torpor, in which my soul had been wallowing, dissipated as the Bible opened spontaneously in the haze of my thoughts to the illuminated page that contains the Sermon on the

Mount; a fiery passage jumped out at me, one which I would have blithely addressed to anyone without even thinking about it, but the cruel truth of which I now penetrated for the first time: "Blessed are the poor in spirit!" This passage continued to haunt me with its aftertaste of coal-tar and iodoform, those leprous odors that evoke death and perpetually bring the viscous fluids from my bowels to the back of my palate, leaving the acid taste of vomit in my throat, while the pulpous mass of someone I cannot call my father moves through the emptiness inside my head . . . .

Madame Gruchet entered through the portal of the transept that was exclusively reserved for Europeans; I immediately felt as if the earth was collapsing beneath my feet.

Despite my good intentions, my efforts, my pious gestures, it was impossible to pray, even though the surroundings invited one to do so: the darkness of the vaulted ceiling, the starry panoply of candle flames, their smell of incense and lepers, the litany of prayers, the hymns, the immense motionless plaster Virgin above the alter, the massive lead crucifix, the images, the nasal wheezing of the antiquated organ . . . . In vain I knelt, placed my face in my hands, pressed my eyelids until I was blinded by flashing spots, got up, knelt again, and began once more . . . all in vain; I was but one wave after another of impatience, burning with desire to ascend the pulpit and silence those fanatical incantations welling from drunken gullets desensitized by alcohol and ricocheting from the arches with the irregularity of a stream bounding frenetically down the side of a mountain. "O-o-o . . . eh-eh-eh-eh! O-o-eh-eh-eh! Ah! Eh-eh-eh . . . O . . . . Yeh-sous!" bawled my neighbor, defeaning me with his onomatopoetic Latin and repeating the Kyrie Eleison, which he sang in his own highly original fashion, so earnestly that one could almost envision the coming of the Lord . . . .

I had regained the dreadful sense of time by asking myself if Marie-Louise, good Christian that she was, could hold out until the end, when she would push open the door upon which my straining eyes were fixed as I silently calculated the distance between myself and it, so I could run up the aisle and take the plunge; if I could only speak to this woman while she was still completely under the spell of her reawakened piety and before she could modestly withdraw her other leg into the automobile and reassume the irritability of a women behind the wheel. I had only to invoke the "Ite, missa est" and ironically discovered I had a greater aptitude than our village chief for enduring the affliction of having to wear his useless gold watch (he didn't believe that anyone could imprison time in the little metal box which the Administration had given him and which he disdained, despised, as a simple ornament that strangled his wrist with "white man's time," so he continued to tell time by the sun in the manner of our ancestors, resting his neck on his left shoulder and squinting his eye like a rogue peering through a keyhole as he repeated to anyone who would listen that only the sky, the sea, and the forest were vast enough to hold his Time), for I found myself glancing at my bare wrist in the shadows, as if I expected to see luminescent watch hands spontaneously materialize beneath the threadbare sleeve of my trench-coat to inform me of the exact second that was perhaps going to convert me into a new man . . . .

Madame Gruchet had not invited me to ride in her car; the door had slammed shut at precisely the moment when my profile had appeared to her through the mist-covered windshield, and I barely had time to jump aside!

Then a gallingly obvious fact dawned upon me: she hadn't seen me; she didn't see me.

It might have ended with that bitter insight, but driven by I don't know what masochistic urge, I would have to follow a long, painful path as the result of tracking my humiliations with the obstinacy of a dog pursuing a scent; I was incapable of feeling absolute hatred toward that woman, whom I naively regarded as another victim of the implacable Order, the cornerstone of which was the fact that we were not friends, that she paid no attention to me. Nevertheless, I told myself that she suffered as a consequence, that she cried into her pillow at night, biting her tongue to keep from betraying the secret of her great love, which I paradoxically assessed as proportional to her indifference. The pleasure of believing against all evidence that she loved me became a vice that I supported by enduring her cruel mortifications.

Six

"They're born sluggards!" That's about all the imperturbable Madame Gruchet must have thought as she saw me dragging myself toward her villa in the rain. She was standing on the other side of the half-opened door, partially sheltered from the gusts of wind that intermittently ballooned her plaid skirt, and she had probably seen me from the bay window in her office, her favorite room, before sitting down to eat; framed in that window were the forest, the large hill, and five hundred meters of a perfectly straight driveway on which she could calmly scrutinize any strangers who ventured into her domain and adjust her expression before hurrying to welcome them on the veranda . . . .

But it was only me, insignificant me, whom she had seen coming into view around the bend—the enormous rain-streaked silhouette of a poor devil whose drenched, mud-splotched, exhausted form, defeated by the rainy season as well as by his lost dreams, was now advancing stiffly toward the villa as if his joints had been frozen. "Him!" she must have exclaimed to herself in irritation, her cheeks livid as she quickly got up to position herself there between the door jamb and the door.

As for me, I hesitated on the doorstep, buffeted by the gusts of wind, and stared at her, without even seeing her at first, for I had attained the peak of an anger that had been painstakingly cultivated during six kilometers of wandering through the rain and the mud, which, for that matter, seemed completely appropriate to my somber reflections while I was lifting one leg after the other with great difficulty, as if they weighed a hundred kilograms and were filled with the dense mercury-like precipitate of an entire year's ridiculous dreams . . . .

I thought the incident at the mission had been a chance occurence that provided me with an excellent opportunity to speak with Madame Gruchet for the first time—to tell her that I had attended mass, that I had seen her, that I had run toward her car, that she had almost run me over,

44

in short, to accuse her and give her a guilty conscience; she would apologize profusely, beg my forgiveness, and her defeat would perhaps enable me to broach the substance of the problem. Yet what if it was a case of aborted revenge on the part of a woman who had never forgiven me for having supplanted her father-confessor in the affairs of her daughter? Convinced that I was in league with her husband and having failed to eliminate me, what would prevent her from shooting me on the spot? Maybe she was concealing a revolver in one of her skirt pockets, where her hands dove for cover, scurried about, and bobbed up and down like little kittens; above all there was her expression—*mama mia*, her expression! What was going to happen to me when confronted by one of those women who are perfectly willing to sacrifice a human life for a simple affair of the heart?

"Ehhh . . . Madmmm . . .!"

My stammering was drowned by the noise of the wind, and blood rushed to my head as the upper part of Madame Gruchet's body stiffened; my heart stopped . . . . Her hands were empty; she had taken them from her pockets to straighten her hair, and after having momentarily heightened my panic to the breaking point, this gesture purged me of it in a single blow.

It was almost noon; at any moment the bugle from the local military camp would sound, sending forth its echoes to expire here; a barechested houseboy was setting the table.

"Well?"

Her skirt was clamped between her thighs, and she made an absurd attempt to smooth down a wisp of hair that the wind once again disheveled.

"I was detained . . . at a funeral." I lied, hoping to arouse her compassion.

"All right!" she said as she glided backwards between the door and the jamb in order to close the door; then she half-disappeared behind the partition and barked at me in a dry voice, the voice of an ill-tempered primary-school teacher. "During the rainy season, you will give your lessons only in the afternoon; my daughter is a bit tired . . . . As far as your salary is concerned, it will be cut in half. You will have to wait until Monsieur returns from his mission before you can get paid [I recalled with a disagreeable sensation that he had just left] . . . . I hope there won't be any more funerals . . . ."

And she shut the door with a bang.

I gnashed my teeth until it seemed as if the enamel were about to splinter . . . . When she slammed the door, I at first had the impression that I was the amalgam of all public solicitors (process-servers, policemen, door-to-door salesmen, beggars), that I had harbored them for a long time

in my soul, and that they were now protesting vehemently; then I suddenly tasted the bilious pleasure of feeling the profound sensation of who
I really was, all alone in that sticky, tenacious mud and mocked by the
hooting of the wind, as if I had just been transported beyond the borders
of a World which, in its course to the stars, had previously ignored this
muddy yet integral part of itself where I had become imbricated—my own
country. And I continued my solitary walk toward the native section of
town . . . .

Seven

Perhaps it was merely a chance occurence, chance having never tired of toying with my insignificant person, which it had once again singled out, prefering me to some European or to anything else that might have served the disconsolate Madame Gruchet as a leaning post, like, for example, those porch columns that she could have clasped in her arms or that hammock in which she loved to stretch out while swinging back and forth; now that it was damp, she could have squeezed and wrung it in sorrow, thereby sparing me an unpleasant misunderstanding. But chance was determined to confound me, to show me its omnipotence, as if I were the greatest miscreant in the world, by stationing me there at precisely the right moment, above the steps on the weather-bleached stoop, fissured by termites or the glancing blows of metallic objects (no one any longer knew which), in the stillness that reigned between periodic gusts of a dormant wind which threatened to renew its attack from one minute to the next; chance had elevated me to that height and placed me in the path of Madame Gruchet's pent-up despair at the very instant when the doctor, whom I saw for the first time in his smock, and a white woman, who was possibly his wife if she wasn't the new European midwife or simply some lady with time on her hands during this tedious season, were taking leave of Madame Gruchet a few steps below me as their car, driven by the lady, bucked with a sudden moan, gained headway, and soon disappeared into the milky drizzle that was falling over the countryside like a felicitous promise of snow . . . .

I no longer knew exactly how it happened; it was so unexpected, and so many things occurred in a fraction of a second that I can't say how Madame Gruchet climbed the three or four steps that separated us in order to throw herself against my chest and cling to my thunderstruck body, transfixed by the proximity of her nearly naked form in a beltless, low-cut, royal blue dressing gown, the neckline of which had been

47

sprinkled with a Lilliputian galaxy of dandruff by a hasty sweep of the comb—a neckline which plunged so deeply that my glance easily passed along the groove in her back to the ground below; she pressed her slightly arched body to mine, and I could see her shoulder blades quiver as they tautened, relaxed, and tautened again like enormous electric oyster shells, raising folds and ripples on a dry skin covered with brownish freckles and responding to some internal tempest, some impetuously uncontrollable force-suction pump that alternately contracted and expanded her insides, distending her stomach in spasms and triggering a succession of waves beneath a flesh that was becoming more and more slippery, more and more fragrant with undefinable exhalations that were alkaline and acidic at the same time, containing hints of garlic and lemon but not completely overwhelming the scent of her usual perfume, while her pulsing skin transmitted its powerful undulations to the marrow of my bones.

What was I to do? Throw this woman to the ground and finish with her immediately (I should have done it already, if I was going to do it at all), or crush her against the wall and take her in a standing position before some intruder could again appear on the scene? There I was, like Elijah in his fiery chariot heading straight to heaven—astonished, embarrassed, and incredulous in the face of what was happening to me . . . . And my glance, which had once again slid with obsessive fixation down the groove of her epileptic back, feverishly tracked imaginary suspicions in the drizzle, out of which loomed the dark mass of the nearby hill and, still closer to us, a quincunx of gloomy sentries formed by the trunks of several palms and firs that stood there like so many open and closed umbrellas . . . . Then, suddenly, it had disappeared all by itself . . . . As far as Madame Gruchet was concerned, she cried and continued to cry with her body plastered against mine in the same position as that of a little girl who might cling to anyone or anything in her despair. Finally, I thought she was going to speak: her voice muffled in sobs, she emitted glottal sounds as if her tongue had been cut off. Theatrically, she tore her head from my chest and stared at me—her face, veiled in tears, was unbearable, causing me to turn my head aside in embarrassment; my body essayed an imperceptible backward movement that she seemed to discern, for I felt her fingernails digging furrows in my arms.

"Forty! Barnabas! [my blood throbbed; she was addressing me so nicely for the first time—me! whose name she had until now disdained to pronounce]. My daughter has a temperature of forty degrees!"*

Ah! That's all it was, and I believed . . . . Then she clutched my hand tightly in hers and led me inside the house.

The sky had suddenly darkened; all that could be heard was the stac-

---

*40 degrees Centigrade is equivalent to 104 degrees Farenheit. (tr)

cato crackle of raindrops tearing at the leaves of the trees. "Too much imagination," I thought as I followed her. She was whimpering and sniffling; she let go of my hand, stepped on my foot while closing the door, passed in front of me again, and, still whimpering and sniffling, held her hands crossed on her chest as she moved with a clip-clopping of sandals to the first door on the left of the hallway that led to the back porch—with a nod of the head, Madame Gruchet beckoned me to follow. I entered that large, austere and sparsely furnished room; unblemished by any sign of masculine disorder, it was the room of a woman who had long ago renounced earthly pleasures and precipitated her daughter into a solitude to which she had eventually become accustomed . . . . The child was lying on her back; I thought she was dead at first, until I saw the covers gently rise and fall to the rhythm of her breathing. I had been disconcerted by her complexion; in the light of the gas lamp that was still burning, her color had turned to the pure white of virgin sheets. Leaning above her daughter, Madame Gruchet was no longer crying; her tears had disappeared by the magic of that astonishing mechanism which a woman's face can sometimes be—a living sponge which brings forth tears and erases them at will; caressing her daughter's face, her hand paused momentarily on a cadaverous temple, and Madame Gruchet no longer moved, no longer breathed. As for me, I was standing behind her and could bear it no longer. "The child is dying," I mused to myself. "She has stopped breathing beneath the covers; it's my own distress that creates the illusion of movement." I felt guilty for not having notified the little girl's parents about her bizarre attitudes.

"Does your foot hurt?" I asked her on the first day.

"No, Monsieur!" she replied, flushing with anger, and as if to mount a diversion, she spontaneously raised her harsh voice to detail the extent of her knowledge.

"And Reverend Father, he was very nice," she added. I wanted to ask her what she meant by that, but I restrained myself; she stared at me with large, frightened eyes . . . . We began the first class. She was intelligent and quite advanced for her age. In whatever subject I questioned her, she responded with a facility that amazed me.

"But you've read everything and retained it all," I blurted out enthusiastically. "There is nothing more to be done with the books we were supposed to be studying until the end of the year. You know them all from beginning to end. We'll have to start on next year's program. In addition, I'll teach you the fundamentals of Greek and Latin. I'm going to make an eminent classicist of you . . . !" I paused; the little girl was looking at me with an irritating coolness in her expression.

"You . . . you aren't happy, Mademoiselle?"

"No! It's not right for my age! Besides, I don't give a damn!"

"Your parents will be proud of you. Maybe they already know."

"They don't know anything at all!"

"You don't want them to know? You don't love them?"

"I love them as much as I hate you!"

My legs were buckling beneath me. My God, what I must seem like to her, I exclaimed to myself. "All the same, I'm going to call your mother," I said.

"I'll tell her you're lying; papa and mama know that all niggers are liars, thieves . . . ."

"Who taught you that? Don't you know that it's a prejudice?"

"Don't care!" She broke into an ironic peel of laughter.

"All right!" I said. "What are we going to do?"

"Nothing!"

"You mean you want me to resign my job and leave? But Latin and Greek are very important . . . ."

"No, it's better for you to earn your money than to go around stealing it. As far as Latin is concerned, I don't give a damn about it either . . . ."

"And what am I going to do to earn my money?"

"We'll stay here. Me, I like it; we can look at the hill . . . ."

She laughed.

"But tell me, what did you do with the Reverend Father? You didn't go over your lessons!"

"It wasn't the same thing."

"Well, well!"

" . . . ."

"What then?"

"You really are annoying me. I told you it wasn't the same thing."

She blushed, lowered her eyes, and began to knead a fold of her dress.

"It's thanks to him that I'm ahead of my class!" she said.

"You didn't understand my question," I continued, returning to the attack. "I'm asking you what you did. Did you work with the other books? I doubt it, because your mother gave me the list and told me to begin with the lessons after the ones the priest had taught you. She herself marked them in red pencil. She wouldn't have taken the trouble, if she knew her daughter had already read them to the end . . . . I'm going to call her in any case, so we can shed some light on this matter . . . ."

She jumped up and said to me, "If you take one step, I'll shout, and Mama will come to chase you away. You're forgetting that I am their only daughter, that you're a nigger, and that my parents will believe everything that I tell them. We'll spend hours here doing nothing, just looking at the hill," she added as she actually looked at it . . . .

"Very well, I said. I wanted to get up and leave, but I was revolted by the thought of retreating in the face of a child.

Then too, I didn't understand what was happening to her. She had collapsed on the desk and was staring at me with the vacant expression of an apoplectic. She was foaming at the mouth and yelping like a dog. Her head was rolling ecstatically as her entire little body shook . . . . I was horrified, and when I approached her, she took her hands out of her dress, turned green, and began to vomit.

"One word about all this, and you're through," she told me between two gasps. In three spasms she threw up her breakfast. Then she ran to tell her mother that she had just vomited.

"It's the climate," proclaimed Madame Gruchet. "This beastly country is not for us, my dear, my treasure." Smothering her child with kisses, she glanced furiously at me, and I felt myself to be the incarnation of an Africa that she hated . . . ."

"That's enough for today!" she commanded.

With trembling hands, I put away the books. As I was descending the stairs, I turned around and encountered the little wench's mocking stare. Yet my passion had proved most resilient. I could not live without seeing Madame Gruchet; the idea of giving up my job made me dizzy and reawakened the dreadful feeling of emptiness that this woman had, without knowing it, enabled me to forget.

"It won't last," said Madame Gruchet as she finally raised herself to her full height; the vials on the bedside table shook and clinked against each other. I felt as if a heavy burden had been lifted from me, and my gaze strayed from the little girl to rest once again where, already the slave of habit, I seemed to belong, but Madame had stood up and was walking toward me, obliging me not to transgress the limits of modesty and obsequiousness I had always maintained between us and thereby compelling me to step backward across the threshold while muttering to myself that the fever had not yet returned to normal, that the child was sleeping; she turned around again to observe her sleeping daughter and quietly closed the door.

We were once again in the hallway; the weather had cleared.

Madame Gruchet opened a window, and the welcome smell of the forest, of the rainy season, filled the house; she sank into an armchair and again began to cry soundlessly. I stood next to her, daring neither to approach too closely nor to sit down. I would have liked to have taken her in my arms, consoled her, stroked her hair. It was not fear, not shyness, that prevented me from doing so, but rather a feeling of impurity that was so viscous and sticky that it made me disgusted with myself . . . . Then I heard Madame Gruchet, who was speaking to me about her daughter's vomit and greenish stools, about her trying night, about her loneliness.

"Shouldn't someone inform Monsieur?" I ventured.

Madame Gruchet, who was sobbing, her face cradled in her hands, suddenly sat up indignantly.

"You know very well that Monsieur is too busy to worry about his family . . . ."

Ah, that tone of voice! How she loved it! How little confidence she had in me! If she had only looked at me, accorded me the least significance, she could never have doubted me. Before I even knew her, hadn't I already loved her—I who was inordinately moved by the fate of this woman, whose indefatigable European husband had taken up residence in the black section of town!

Her daughter called her. She bounded up and ran into the room. Although I dared not follow her up there again, I did advance as far as the hallway; a few minutes later she emerged, relaxed, happy, and with a perceptible urge to jump for joy.

"Her temperature has gone down . . . . Everything will be back to normal tomorrow . . . ."

Then it was as if she suddenly descried me; she didn't seem to understand what I was doing there. She gave a start, straightened the top of her dressing gown, and hurriedly crossed her hands in front of her chest. A tinge of red rose to her cheeks. She had readopted that aggressive and irritating mood of the naive young girl she no longer was, except in the backward image of time, as if I had come lusting after something that was still no more than a pipe-dream. She tried to smile, no doubt recalling at last the tense moments we had just experienced together. She was sufficiently distraught to assure me once again that our patient was doing better. I headed for the door, which she allowed me to open. It was still raining . . . . Then, without detaining me, that woman, who was not kind and whose face had assumed all the infinite nuances of a person betrayed by her mood and now doing her utmost to regain her composure, suddenly experienced the desire to speak with me, overwhelming me with incoherent pronouncements. As I walked away, I heard her honoring me a bit too late with her plans.

Eight

My mother entered my room and sat down on my bed, drawn there by her unhappiness, as in the old days when we were still living with my father. Her presence evoked a bitter-sweet emotion in me. But such phantoms from the past vanished immediately as the herald-of-the-white-man's-pleasures intoned his appeals, disturbing the oppressive, humid silence of the black neighborhood. He announced that a European had arrived at the rest house and wanted a woman for the night, "An opportunity, my sisters! An op-por-tun-i-ty!" Embarrassed, we heard his voice move away and then fall silent near the catechist's hut; he had seven daughters . . . .

My mother's cough caught me by surprise, and I imagined, not without regret, that she was moping in a peevish uncertainty, not knowing exactly what to say and perhaps enjoining herself from believing that I had returned to her for good after the touching evening we had just spent together.

I had dashed into the house like a whirlwind during the dry season, animatedly popping up here, there, and everywhere as I imparted my giddiness to her; before she could recover from her astonishment, I had grabbed my towel, plucked a banana, and begun running in the rain toward the river, shouting to her that she should get ready to go to the movies.

In this country where they show nothing but Westerns, we had the extraordinary good luck to happen upon a Louis Jouvet film that we experienced, alas, a great deal of difficulty in following, since Pathé-Journal's superb cock provoked among our neighbors a strong urge to prattle on like chickens, and for that reason they took the liberty of recounting to each other in loud voices the memories of their own agapes.

Although she didn't understand the French, my mother had been enchanted by the love story; we rehashed it on the way back until I noticed that my mother, who had until then taken a lively interest, was no longer following my comments; she suddenly seemed preoccupied. She walked the rest of the way home in silence to the plashing rhythm of our feet as they splashed through the invisible pools of the night.

I would probably have returned to my room without saying a word and then fallen into the profound sleep that usually rescued me from boredom, if my mother, unable to wait any longer, had not decided to come and sit down on my bed. I was lying on my back, observing her from beneath the arm that lay across my face. I was furious at having given my mother a pleasure that my own instability was incapable of sustaining for long.

"I'm a bad son!" I finally stated with a bluntness that might have resembled an onset of sincere repentence, although at that very instant I was actually angry with her, perhaps even reproaching her for being my mother.

"I'm a failure, a nonentity!" I continued. "Up to now what have I done that's worthwhile in my life? I can't even succeed in giving you the simple happiness of a mother who knows that she is loved by her son. Why do I have to be bored by everything?"

But my mother didn't react; she had a unique capacity to become simply the absence of life as soon as her instinct told her that I was going to hurt her, that she was going to suffer once again . . . .

Emboldened in the end by my own monologue, I told her I had decided to leave for Europe, for France—"the only country where I can 'realize' myself."

She replied without spite or bitterness that "I was right . . . and with a bit of luck . . ."

I didn't understand any longer; not that I felt frustrated by her despair, but I was adrift—how could my mother sever our moorings like this with a single stroke of renunciation and without appearing in the least to be dissembling! I would have preferred everything to happen as it had before: she exploding in anger, launching into insinuations, or smiling, all of which would have given me the opportunity to slam the door in her face while placing the blame on her bad character.

However, my mother was quite determined to prove herself sublime. She told me that I had had a "very good idea" and that retaining me by her side in this country would never give her the happiness of seeing me become "a successful nigger." Times having changed, it was necessary to take the initiative, to create one's own chances, devise one's own luck; of course she would suffer a great deal as a result of being separated from me for a long time, but that was unavoidable . . . . "I won't die between now and then," she asserted passionately. "God could not be that unjust!" Then she surveyed the list of people who might be able to help us. "Why don't you write to the Government—you who know how to write French so well—and ask them to send you to France? You could even include a bit of Latin to impress them! That way they'll send out someone to look for the chap who was bright enough to mail them such a letter . . . ." In her naive, girlish enthusiasm, she had spoken without taking a breath, until, disabused, she pulled herself together and declared herself a fool. "Who knows us up there?" she added. "Even so, that won't prevent you from going to France—you're going to succeed; it was like this when I had a premonition of your success in that important examination the white men made you take . . . ."

"But we don't have anything, mama," I told her, "not a thing with which to pay for the surety bond, the ticket, my wardrobe, and my tuition for many years of study in a country where, it seems, you have to pay for everything, even the simple natural pleasures of sitting down or pissing!"

"I should have known," she said after a moment's pause. "That's why all those white men preferred to come here, where everything is free . . . ."

"It isn't that, mama . . . ."

"Then it's the poor whites who have come here, those who can't sit down or piss in their own country . . . ? And that's why they're as merciless as the slave in the Bible!"

". . . ."

"Now I'm certain you're going to become somebody in their country; the bad ones are here, whereas over there they only have good white men who will help you; you'll make friends, you'll study, then you'll come back . . . ."

"But don't you really understand that I don't have anything? It's merely an idea that occurred to me once; I'm not even thinking about it any more."

"We'll go to all the villages in the tribe; I'll speak to those bush niggers! Leave it to me! When you come back, they'll no longer say, 'it's so-and-so's son,' but rather, 'he's from such-and-such a tribe!' Well then, they have to do something for the glory that redounds to them. I'll speak to them, and Vavap, that old clown of an Ancestor, can't refuse us; all he has to do is say, 'we have decided to send this young man to France,' and you will be on your way . . . . We'll go to all the villages in the tribe; Vavap will understand us . . . ."

"Yes, Mama! We'll speak to them . . . ."

"That's no reason to cry like a girl," she admonished me in a virile tone of voice that I had not heard before. In the darkness, she stood up, a delicate moving shade among the motionless shadows; she leaned over, kissed me on the forehead, and wished me a good night. Then with a gentle shuffling of her bare feet, she moved away, mechanically avoiding bits of half-burned wood and the utensils that had been left here and there on the floor of our furniture-less hut, until she reached the hanging mat that separated our rooms; I heard her brush it aside and then draw it back again behind her. Finally, she sat down on her bed, and it creaked. She didn't lie down on it; time passed, and not a sound could be heard, except the teeming of raindrops on the thatched roof and the croaking of frogs in a nearby pond; the houseboy of a few moments ago and the Negress for the night must have been staggering like two blind drunkards down the other side of the ridge that marked the border between our section of town and that of the Europeans, while the white man at the rest house must have been keeping watch in his pyjamas as he nervously smoked one cigarette after another, from time to time resting his elbows on the window sill and casting alternately optimistic, angry, and despairing glances at his watch as he paced like a caged animal from his look-out post to the whiskey bottle that kept him company, but without daring to venture into this pitch-black night and onto the fine asphalt street where his car gleamed in the shadows and his hopes lay concealed. No, he dared not go out to meet them; he must have noticed the indispensible topographical map hanging in the drawing room, and it indicated that this street leads to the native settlement, where he had sent the houseboy, and then progressively degenerates into a track, a fetid rivulet, as it approaches our neighborhood . . . .

Finally, my mother moved—a very faint creaking of her bamboo bed followed by a long silence; I sensed that she was not going to sleep at all during the night, and it was in vain that I pricked my ears to discern the usual jingling of her bracelets sliding down to her elbows as she raised her arms and the heavy breathing that always accompanied her efforts to pull her dress over her head with a barely audible snapping of threads (she resewed them each morning) and a rustling of fabric, all those sounds that served as a prelude to her falling asleep. I could imagine her as tense, holding in her breath, sitting stiffly on the edge of the bed; the faint sound a few moments before had undoubtedly betrayed the movement of her legs, which she had wanted to draw carefully back to the edge of the bed before leaning forward and, heels raised, placing her weight on her toes as she awaited an outside noise—the rumbling of thunder, for example—to stand up, tear herself away from that indiscreet bed in a single movement, and go behind the hut to cry . . . .

Nine

To obtain the aid of the tribe, we thus went to solicit the support of Fimsten Vavap, an illiterate, lascivious old man who could nevertheless transform himself into a formidable preacher. Thought to be the last living descendent in the long line of great ancestors, he benefited from their legendary renown, purged of all stains and transfigured by the scintillating diamond lens of their posthumous glory, from which an entire people drew sustenance . . . . They say that the words of God issued through this old man's mouth and that his sanction would suffice for the tribe to bestow upon me in hard cash the viaticum that was so necessary for my trip to France . . . .

We took a bush taxi on the road that leads toward the sea—a laterite ribbon that twists into the distance between embankments containing the grizzly remains of fatal accidents. Banana trees, giant ferns, the forest, and the underbrush all tend to smother this narrow red strip of bare earth. The air is dank and fetid. Enormous palms obscure the sun, and even during the dry season, the drone of passing vehicles becomes as humid as at the height of the rains. Picked clean by the *magnans,** piles of chimpanzee or gorilla bones lie bleaching here and there like the skeletons of children. Even the wild animals seem to have been bitten by the tse-tse fly— antelope graze peacefully without appearing to notice the momentary din, which is only remarked by a wretched but jovial humanity that comes occasionally into view, naked groups flashing pearly smiles behind friendly waves of the hand and gathered in front of hovels, heaps of dried mud framed by twin cemeteries that are no more than fields of pockmarked excrescences inhabited by rats as big as cats and sprinkled with dilapidated, rotting crosses which bear the tiny veins of termite colonies and the burden of dried palm fronds . . . .

---

*An extremely voracious variety of red ants.

57

Vavap's father had been paraded along this route by the Germans, who had placed a rope around his neck before deciding to hang him from an umbrella tree, from which they forbade Vavap, under pain of death, to take down the corpse. Vultures, hawks, eagles, and crows feasted upon it until a storm dispersed his bones through the surrounding forest. It seems that's why this region became so desolate and gruesome . . . .

The village was virtually deserted when we arrived. Only the old men and children put in an appearance, and at first I saw no more than his feet, molded into strips of old automobile tires: they were swinging on either side of a hammock. Bare-chested and holding one hand around his herniated navel, which I, embarrassed and outraged, at first mistook for his sexual organ, Vavap slept, or appeared to be sleeping, above his peers, who might well have been imitating him, although one could hardly judge the matter with certainty. A fine young girl with breasts like the thorny spikes of a baobab kept away the flies by nonchalantly fanning him with a branch. From time to time she was also supposed to fill and pass around a single dirty enamel goblet that was chipped in spots and lacked a handle, resembling a chamber pot more than a utensil from which anyone might want to take a refreshing draught. This group of senile old men dozing in the shade of the house of palaver in the middle of the deserted little village gave rise to such an impression of sadness and boredom that I was overcome by the desire to persuade my mother that it would be better to turn back . . . . But the young woman had stood up, and her hand was already reaching toward the old man's bulbous, wrinkled, varicose-vein-furrowed stomach when my mother's cough forestalled her. The Notables opened their eyes. I became ill at ease in the presence of that bald-headed man. His eyes, which appeared to have been pierced with a compass, betrayed not the slightest flash of brightness; his pupils resembled tiny goat turds screwed into his purulent yellow sclera. He yawned; a single mucid molar, hypertrophied by tartar, appeared like a glob of bilious spittle at the back of his empty palate. Then, having sat up astraddle in his hammock, he smiled roguishly at my mother and clasped his hands as he coughed lightly a few times, incapable of dissimulating the interest he suddenly took in her by flaunting the false modesty of a man who was sure of himself but did not want to reveal his intentions in order to gain his interlocutor's sympathy; all the women of the tribe took a sacred pleasure in sharing this old man's bed, and he, having convinced himself of his irresistibility, undoubtedly thought that my mother too . . . . He had imprisoned one of her hands in his own and was kneading it as he inquired about news from the town. The other old men regarded them with exaltation, aiming the double barrels of their snot-and-snuff filled noses toward the pair and rolling their sparkling eyes from one side to the other of their orbits. It made me want to puke! Was mama an accomplice to this scene, or was she being indulgent for reasons of diplomacy? I no longer knew where to rest my eyes. I turned around and must have muttered some obscenity, because my indignant mother immediately stopped joking; the old men fell silent, and she ordered me in a jarring tone of voice to come pay my respects to the Notables. "This is my son," she informed them. Fimsten Vavap opened his arms wide. Well, what then? Did I really have a bad character? Wasn't Vavap merely playing at being a Notable? Under duress, I submitted to his phlegmy embrace, which cost me a terrible prickling in my nostrils at the touch of his clammy skin—he whom I would have greeted, maybe, with no more than a discreet brush of hands now hastened to grasp one of mine in his, imprisoning it between his horny palms as he had done to my mother, thus creating an equivocal situation in my mind and rendering him all the more sublime, because he had originally impressed me as a slimy old bastard. But I guarded myself against this change of course, which would have generated a distressing ambiguity in me, by reflecting that the warmth of his welcome for me was but a sham to assuage my suspicions; for this reason, the idea occurred to me that I should force the issue! I urged my mother to tell him the purpose of our visit, so that we would not miss the bush taxi. The effect was what I had anticipated: the old men exploded. They all tried to speak at once, but Vavap's voice dominated the assembly. "How can you who have nothing, you who are nothing at all, demand that we feel an obligation to do your bidding?" He then launched into a violent diatribe against my generation, which he characterized as the plague of the country, the curse of God. With a visible nostalgia, the patriarch undertook to recount the origins of the tribe, exalting the temperament of each generation since that of warriors who could pride themselves upon having relished the luxury of spitting in their enemy's face before plunging their poisoned spears into his flank and gallantly wrapping his guts around the metal part of their weapons, leaving the entrails to smoke in the sun "like those long things people eat in town . . . ," but now all that is changed, he went on; in the old days, there was a pact between the Tribe and Nature—it had assumed the habit of manifesting itself at each birth by donning one of its thousand faces, a face that, like fate, supposedly marked the children of any given generation. But the universe had remained impassive when this generation of good-for-nothings arrived on the scene, this curse-ridden generation that dares defy paternal authority while offending Heaven and the Whites, whose fearful reprisals it is possible to foresee . . . .

These words had the virtue of triggering in my mother one of those reactions that are essentially dictated by her instinct: she immediately took my side, and with an uncompromising look on her face, her eyes reduced to narrow slits, and her neck stretched forward, she advanced slowly toward the hammock. She exploded, "I don't like people speaking to my son that way!" And the old man, who must not have understood what was happening to him, to him who had for a long time been spared the haughty, jealous, aggressive, passionately angry or snivellingly self-pitying moods of the tribe's women, from whom he exacted a tranquil pleasure with the benediction of their complacent husbands—this old man suddenly became pitiful, collapsing on his back in fright as if he had just been felled by the kick of an enemy steed.

"I . . . ," I wanted to retort.

"Be quiet!" my mother commanded me. "We didn't come here to listen to such tales . . . . The Tribe! The Tribe! All right then! Let's see what it can do. Let it send this young man to the white man's country, where he can become somebody and then return to his people!"

"Oh, woman! Oh, simpleton!" replied the old man. "Does your son need to go to the white man's country to become somebody in the tribe? What about me? Have I ever crossed seas and mountains to become He who I am? Doesn't your son, who can speak French like a white man, or a white ninny, and who, it seems, can also understand the language of the priests—doesn't he know enough already? When will he work like a good son and take his turn at providing for you? Oh woman! Oh, simpleton! Does one need that much to succeed in life?"

And he deliberately prolonged his oration, lending it such scope and profundity that the old man himself actually attained a certain grandeur in my eyes as he vibrated in harmony with the words he was intoning in his ecstatic torpor. But the effect they produced in my mother's biased soul was precisely the opposite of that anticipated by the "Ancestor"; he had sought to take advantage of his good faith, his experience, his age, and his authority to discourage us, while at the same time heaping praise upon me, but my mother only had ears for the latter, and Vavap realized it with an inward wrath that caused him to roll his eyes impatiently. He was no longer certain whether it was wise to persist in this form of discouragement by reference to the absurd, for he only succeeded in brightening the impudent expression on the face of this forty-year-old town woman, who was now fueling her pride with the reputation which her son had heretofore acquired as a scholar and which he, Vavap, the Notable of Notables, was offering to consecrate in spite of himself. Nevertheless, he believed that in doing so, he was reining in the disturbing ambition of this young man, who seemed quite intent upon crossing the world's oceans to fashion for himself a foreign reputation that would subsequently allow him to return and put an end to the rule of the Notables. He was certainly capable of it, this nonentity who was staring brazenly at him! Well, then, what could he say to make them renounce their plans?

"It is very sad," he sighed, "that death is not the twin sister of absence, for then we might someday hope to see our children return from abroad

. . . . Oh, youth which fears nothing! Will you ever know the tears you occasion . . . ."

I would indeed have liked to answer him, but on the other side of the compound I glimpsed a woman bent double beneath an enormous basket of provisions that she was carrying back from the fields. I then felt intensely the sadness and boredom latent in the bad mood that had afflicted me ever since we had come into the presence of this collection of old men who were dying outside of time and entreating me not to leave the country, not to emigrate to Europe—old men undoubtedly motivated as much by a morbid concern for their own impotent authority as by an exaggerated pessimism in regard for my future, and even when they invoked the uncertainty of our ever seeing each other again, it was not, as one may have surmised, a reflection of that excessive bitterness characteristic of aging individuals depressed by an obsession with death, but rather, on the contrary, an expression of their lugubriously naive egotism; it was actually the possibility of my death in a foreign country that was troubling them.

"Think about your parents, about the tribe, about all of us who are perhaps seeing you for the last time. Think about your mother, who has no one but you in the whole world . . . . Who will bury you over there in the white man's country? Remember that we will not even have the consolation, the final consolation of seeing your remains and mourning . . . ."

Those were the last words intoned by Vavap in his night bird's voice, and all that remained for us was the expedient of running to avoid missing the bush taxi.

Ten

Poor, without relatives or friends, and ridiculed for my dreams, I would not, however, allow myself to be discouraged. I must confess that I was a Hydra of chimeras, a monster of optimism in a country where man had been dehumanized by the appetite for power and profit and by the cult of selfishness.

People told me, "Africa is becoming respectable; your Latin is still a valuable asset; you already know enough to become someone here! Why dream only of going to France? Enter the race; look at those who are reaching the top! Political connections will soon prevail over diplomas . . . . Be careful! You still seem to be waiting for something. You have to make up your mind."

But as for me, I knew what I was waiting for: the reply to a long letter (twenty densely-packed, handwritten pages in which I had recounted the story of my life) that I had addressed to the Governor in the hope of obtaining a fellowship to study in France. ". . . To be more useful to our country and to France," I had concluded, but not before adding "Long live Africa," and "Long live France," and "Long live the Franco-African Community," all in ornate capital letters scaled to reflect my enthusiasm.

My soul at peace, I sealed the envelope and then, rejoicing in the prospect of sailing across oceans, standing on a third-class deck, impervious to the rolling of the ship and an exhilarating sea-sickness that served as a pleasant reminder of my having actually departed, my avid gaze lost in the foggy, liquid immensity of the sea, I pursued the Europe of my dreams, that Western World refulgent with sunsets into which gulls were continuously flying . . . .

I ran to the post office, bought the stamps, feverishly affixed them to the still damp corner I had licked in advance, and, as if to guarantee them a certain permanence on the spot, pounded them with a powerful twisting blow of the fist; then, with a slight show of emotion, I slipped the letter into the box . . . . I remained there, motionless, incapable of leaving, of moving away, overcome by an indefinable sadness.

As I awaited a reply, I forswore the search for a new job, allowing myself a delectable vacation after the brief expression of gratitude with which the Gruchets had honored me and which—upon my word—was accompanied by a tolerably well-filled envelope; under pressure from a husband intent upon recovering his freedom. Madame had decided to return to France. She naively hoped he would soon rejoin her there . . . .

My mother had become engaged in the clandestine manufacture of corn alcohol, and that iniquitous branch of trade sufficed to feed us. I could finally consort with young people my own age. To be sure, I was often subject to sudden fits of prudishness and last-minute equivocations that resulted only in turning scholarship to ridicule on the basis of my example, for viewed from the perspective of my comrades' spontaneity and uncompromising bluntness, I was no more than an idle dullard, a hair-splitting pedant whose fate consoled them for never having become neurotically indecisive Latinists and whose least show of pride they unhesitatingly treated with disdain; however, out of spite and a kind of desperate braggadocio, I wormed my way with apparent equanimity into their noisy, half-starved, shabbily-dressed group that never tired of swaggering across the top of the butcher-shop stairs, from whence we appraised the usual fauna of market places, our necks craned and oscillating like pendulums that swept from one end of the little square to the other in quest of a billfold that some careless chap might absent-mindedly stuff into a hip-pocket . . . . Sometimes we delighted in the painful flinch of an addlepated, elephantine native gendarme, who suddenly spun on his heels, his eyes starting out of his head in a futile attempt to locate the source of an invisible dart that had just harpooned one of the fleshy arcs protruding from his amphibian posterior . . . .

Not to become unworthy of the high honor solicited from the Governor, unless it was out of fear that I might find myself with a shaved head reflecting the sun and a khaki uniform that consisted primarily of a collarless, sleeveless, buttonless shirt—a sort of chasuble which was adorned on the front and back with a large coal tar "P" and which, on me, would have fallen below the knees, completely engulfing a miniscule pair of tiny shorts, so tiny that people would have felt the urge to crouch down on the ground, as if confronted with a pair of kilts, to convince themselves that there was indeed something else beneath it—while carrying a shovel on my shoulder and swelling the chorus of prisoners, which, growing steadily with more and more recruits from our group, paraded through the streets of the Business District during peak hours, singing obscene praises to the sexual glory of Olinga,* who marched at the head of their column, I

---

*A guard particularly well-known in the area for his brutality.

deserted the butcher-shop stairs in favor of the enclosed courtyard in front of the Hôtel de France. This large imitation rococo structure dominated the east side of the market-place, and although, with the exception of civil servants and politicians, we natives entered it only with occasional glances, an anonymous, peaceful band of idlers and flunkeys, reduced to unemployment by age, the death or departure of a patron, or a few recurrent peccadillos, was always milling aimlessly about in front of it. With a certain sadness, they came to flaunt their heart-breaking availability, their oppressive freedom, in the shade of this impressive edifice that they flattered with large pearly or toothless smiles, raising their fists in the vain hope that someone might deign to arrest them, revealing the extent to which they lacked a former notoriety that had made them feared as merciless slaves in the native township or in their villages. Glued to the hotel steps that served the European fauna from the interior as an ashtray and a spitoon—a fauna, incidentally, that could pride itself upon never having suffered its rheumy spittle to touch the ground in this corner of the world—these pitiful creatures jabbered away, laughed, told each other stories from morning until evening, argued over cigarette butts or kola nuts, and dashed off in all directions as soon as the owner emerged with a club in his hands. All of which had not the slightest effect upon the powdered and painted Negresses of all sizes and ages; they were "permit ladies" or "Commissioner's ladies," as people indiscriminantly referred to them. Like the taxis parked nearby, they were tacitly and permanently available until the wee hours of the morning, waiting for the last European, the last possible well-fed customer, to stagger from the hotel and either gratify their daily hope ever so little or dash it completely with a vulgar insult. They constituted a standing affront to the local male population, furious that these lost women had rebelled sexually against them, while cynically introducing eccentricities like straight hair, wigs, lipstick, cigarette holders, and a predilection for pants as a prelude to their plan for imitating their European rivals and emancipating themselves from the inhuman servitude of the African woman.

Intrigued by these traitoresses as much as I was attracted to them, I finally succeeded, after three months of witticisms, humiliations, boasts, and bribes, in gaining the problematic affections of the least indomptible of that indomptible sect. Her name was Anatatchia; a soft, pulpous mass of flesh, she had become subject, since having been relieved of her ovaries, to the unlimited growth of all castrated beasts, and although she was insufferable on account of her bad French, that pidgin French in which she insisted upon whispering endearments to me, everything would still have turned out for the best between us, as time and habit intended, if Anatatchia, for whom I was, according to her, the first black lover, had not persisted in her attempt to reeducate my impulses so they might correspond with those of the "Other"—a certain Lieutenant Lapasse, whose arcane caprices she had herself inherited. And then there was her tendency to remind me of the value of what she was offering me at the very moment when I was incapable of replying or even tendering a verbal testimony of my gratitude. She adopted the habit of remaining silent in a nervous expectancy that I could easily terminate by chirping in her ear that she had made a privileged nigger of me.

In the end I realized that I had developed an inexhaustible patience for putting up with this saucy wench, who was obsessed with her European admirers and especially that aged officer, whose name passed her lips as frequently as her daily bread.

One day as we were arguing over my eyes—she had such a strange way of sucking on them that I recoiled each time for fear they would flow like eggs into the ardent, roiling gulf of the bulbous mouth that was eagerly breathing them in—Anatatchia had the gall to burst into laughter before informing me once again in a soft, mysterious tone of voice that "he loved it!" I took advantage of the situation to finally get some things off my chest. So much the worse for me; she possessed a talent that verged on genius for humiliating repartee, and having thrown my pants into the courtyard (fortunately it was dark), she pushed me after them, intimating that I was no longer to venture into her abode and ignoring me from that moment on . . . .

The need to see her again impelled me to spy on her from a distance. Concealed behind a tree or a house, I could watch her strolling about, wriggling her hips, in the enclosed courtyard at the Hôtel de France, where every Thursday evening a bus driven by a talkative young Greek unloaded whites who were enamored of an imaginary Africa they apparently had come to explore only so they could lock it up in picture albums destined to fire the imaginations of those adventure-starved, arm-chair travelers who abound in bourgeois Europe.

These champions of adventure came in both sexes and all ages, arriving breathless and with beaming faces in our part of the world. It was almost as if a factory had disgorged them here, their craning necks hung with the obligatory case of a camera that would later be attached to the eye, thereby immobilizing their faces in an imperceptible dumb show beneath the shadow of their emormous pith helmets. Programmed in advance and steeped in a facile enthusiasm that breaks out in the face of unfathomable darkness like the violent onset of a storm whenever they encountered some poor devil, a monkey, a naked woman, or a madman, they were constantly on the alert, perpetually in quest of rituals, always ready to remove the tops from their pens, to track down a savage, the real savage of their youthful fantasies, the "Bamboula"* who had remained unmarked by the passage of time, and to write a book, the great book which had never before been written about this part of the world and the title of which ricocheted from the corrugated metal roof along with the corks of champagne bottles as they discussed this continent, whose unique and inexpressible character they were all so well qualified to comprehend and explain!

And in a mercenary sort of way, I became their local guardian angel, who enabled them to photograph or film a pygmy, a monkey swinging from its branch, a boa swollen by its painful digestion, a hippopotamus lumbering away from the river bank, an indigenous marriage in which the bride and bridegroom approach each other while wagging their heads to the rhythm of a balaphon—so many scenes that are "tremendous," "remarkable," and "sensational"! My fellow tribesmen also improvised a ritual for us whenever my explorers were willing to pay the "matabish," usually the price of several demijohns of red wine or palm wine, with which the unemployed, starveling actors drank themselves into a stupor before feverishly staging their production as the spectators smiled at the thought of the next film festival, where they were going to overwhelm the jury and snatch from them the Grand Prize that would consecrate them as Africanists.

Official guide at the Hôtel de France, I was finally able to take up a post inside that imposing edifice, to which I had been introduced with a resounding smack on the shoulder by the red-haired Monsieur Hébrard, a powerful, hirsute Alsatian. For my use, he had arranged a little office directly across from the cash register, where his wife kept watch with the vigilance of Cerberus; she was an enormous Alsatian woman, who loved canned sauerkraut and the dark beer that she quaffed at every opportunity from a glass placed next to her adding machine. Made dizzy by watching her turn constantly in all directions while chewing absentmindedly, I finally came to the conclusion that she had three heads.

My office was perched on a stage built for an orchestra that Monsieur Hébrard had never been able to constitute according to a plan abandoned several years after the end of the Second World War (which he had valiantly fought somewhere else), because he had at long last modernized his establishment by installing electricity and running water. The former permitted him to introduce the town's first record-player, which in turn enabled him to dispense with those phlegmatic, undisciplined, illiterate,

---

*Originally a primitive African drum and the dance that was performed to the beating of it, the word "Bamboula" acquired pejorative connotations in French (c.f., "nigger"), in part through conflation with "bamboche" (a large puppet or stunted, deformed individual). (tr)

bizarre, and quite possibly syphilitic black musicians who would have delighted his clientele, if they had not stupidly insisted upon remaining loyal to their filthy hovel in the native township under fallacious, childish, and even quite vexing pretences like the interminably steep hill between the black and the white sections of town—an obstacle they cited to legitimize their refusal, although they were hardly old men susceptible of dying at the least exertion; it was all the more exasperating in light of the fact that Monsieur Hébrard had shown himself more than generous in offering them an amount that would have enabled them to dedicate themselves to their aging instruments until the end of their days.

I thus found myself once again a preacher without a congregation on this stage, which had been indemnified for its barrenness with numerous cases of Alsatian beer and which now offered me a vantage point from which my peripatetic gaze occasionally landed upon the flesh-clogged furrow in Madame Hébrard's throat that glistened with humidity as she glanced for a fraction of a second in the opposite direction; it was one of the most caricaturable traits of this woman, who would certainly have appealed to Dubout* when the powerful fantail of her enormous pallid thighs spread her skirt and yawned through the lozenge-shaped mesh beneath the counter. I could see her sitting below me, always damp, chewing, drinking, swearing, gossiping, and grumbling from one end of the day to the other as she vociferated against God, the Devil, her aging native assistants, and her own flea-bitten crotch (she was constantly clutching it and scratching it with an unpleasant rasping of fingernails on the fabric of her skirt), or the foaming beer in a large, ribbed glass that, refilled countless times each day, stood within easy reach of her bloated hand, covered with blotches and bulging with greasy fat; she drank her beer in lengthy draughts to quell the unquenchable thirst that had afflicted her since menopause. At every moment she railed coarsely against her ironic fate as a matronly barkeeper in the African bush—she who had come with her husband twenty-one years previously to spend but a short time there, only enough time for her to become a great lady, one of those with cars, yachts, furs, jewelry, lovers, scandals—like the celebrities upon whose escapades she childishly nourished in her dreams, for that was how she remained abreast of international affairs in the depths of a virgin forest, where those mindless women's magazines reached her regularly, albeit with considerable delay; she had subscribed to them at the beginning and renewed her subscription each year with great enthusiasm. But time had passed, and Madame Hébrard, who had only endured life in this God-forsaken country in the hope of becoming a great lady in Europe, had finally realized the truth at an age when neither mirrors nor men any

---

*A popular twentieth-century French cartoonist. (tr)

longer gave her reasons to believe in illusions, with her vast posterior amply overflowing either side of the stool that penetrated the cleft between her thighs, with her complexion that was simultaneously swarthy, green, ruddy, and pallid according to location, with her sticky, graying hair that rolled permanently across her temples as if it had been spit out by a wood plane, the result of an unflagging diligence in coifing her skull with curlers every night for twenty-one years before going to bed in a country where, without hairdressers, one is obliged to do everything for one's self; Madame Hébrard had finally realized that the climate, alcohol, miscarriages, illnesses, and all the evils of life in the colonies were in the process of transforming her, by means of a cruel and Machiavellian alchemy, into a sort of ochre Negress, although she unconsciously resisted the comparison by randomly humiliating and disparaging her authentic sisters who plied their trade on all sides of her establishment. And I imagined her undressing angrily each night in front of a mirror, imprisoned in the solitude of her room on the first floor—her husband maintained a separate bedroom in a villa near the garage on the grounds of the concession; he brought her there occasionally, not for reasons that one might have suspected, but just simply "to discuss matters for an instant" in private without the presence of natives, the couple's intimacy serving only to frustrate our curiosity about their disputes, although the tart voice of Madame Hébrard reached us through the walls of the room whenever her husband, who was carrying on two affairs in the European part of town, began to fleece her, to tap her for money. Never did a woman scream so much like a stuck pig as she did at the sight of her handsome, fifty-year-old husband with his smooth forehead and silver temples, which fate utilized in this way to avenge us upon his wife, a venemous creature who was quick to bite and inflict pain. She fulminated endlessly against her trio of aging native domestics appareled all in white, including white caps that sank into their greying hair and sprouting points above their ears like the chalk-colored pastry horns of xylaphogous termites, giving them, in conjunction with the gravity and sadness that chronic misery inscribes on disillusioned faces, the false appearance of intellectuals or scholars. For twenty-one years they had been scampering from one end of the bar to the other in the arduous, dignified, yet ridiculous race of fat men who are perpetually late—a little race they endlessly recommenced until the late-night closing time, periodically displaying the contrast between their still snowy-white teeth and the dull, blood-stained whites of their eyes in the cramped space of the vulgar ellipse clearly deliniated by the eagle eye of the woman who governed their movements by constantly swiveling above the arsenious grey of the adding machine. Hoary with age, these black men had probably logged the equivalent of a trip around the world by dint of rushing interminably back and forth along the five or six meters of the bar under the protuberant surveillance of Madame Hébrard.

Years ago, brimming with the hope of succeeding and starting their own business by capitalizing upon their zealousness at the Hôtel de France, they had performed, and continued to perform, their duties with an extraordinary nobility beneath the strict governance of that indecently charming woman that Madame Hébrard, fascinating to them in proportion to her unattainability, must have been. They accorded themselves no respite. They felt compelled to keep busy, to work, to move about, to do anything that might have prompted Madame Hébrard to display the gold-silver-ivory expanse of her teeth in a mouth that never smiled unless it was in her interest to do so. And since the shops only filled with customers during certain hours of the day, my aging fellow countrymen were obliged to invent other tasks in the interim; I could see them jump over the bar and noticed the stocky, long-suffering, abnormally swollen calves of their legs, on which the varicose veins of patience seemed ready to burst, threatening to rip apart their smooth black skin. And the calves of these legs frantically scaled the wheel, then the body of trucks parked in front of the establishment and waiting to be unloaded under the mocking eye of workers who supervised such operations; after ascending skyward, the calves disappeared, only to reappear a moment later, more swollen than ever, and repeat the procedure in reverse, creating the impression that they were the sole organs supporting the monumental burdens with which my old fellows were burdened. Sweating and gasping for breath but content with themselves, the trio reentered the bar without a break to embark once again upon their customary little race along the counter, drumming on it with pudgy fingers that the perpetual washing of dishes had transmuted into the ashen grey of a black corpse that had been left in the river for a long time. They only interrupted this same little race which, it must be added, they immediately resumed, when the boss relaxed the folds in her neck to roar at me with all the rancor that a woman like her can inject into her voice, shouting a "good-for-nothing lazybones" that put an abrupt end to my reverie.

She was right, Madame Hébrard; ever since I had begun living only in my dreams of Paris, I led a somnambulistic existence, and the profession I exercised in her domain was hardly suited to remedy that state of affairs; it was the sort of job that consisted solely of sitting and waiting, the sort of job in which the virus of idleness eventually triumphs over even the most honest people, and since I did not figure among their number, I once again found myself completely at ease, sprawling across a case of beer and daydreaming about what the lives of Madame Hébrard and her assistants might have been, when her barking woke me with a start. So I pretended to gather up the topographical maps of the surrounding countryside, through which I had the mission of piloting all those Africanists who had been ferried to our shores by Europe and America. I was later to re-encounter many of these gentlemen, who regarded Africa as their private preserve, in France where they had carved out impressive reputations for themselves. Ah, yes, those gentlemen whom I had the honor of piloting through the bush, through my native forest! Nothing but walking Encyclopedias, intellectual giants whose honesty, integrity, and duly consecrated sense of self-sacrifice prevented them from paying the slightest attention to the vulgar and mundane necessity of replenishing a depleted bank account when, defying the climate, the malaria, the dysentery that were lurking in ambush for them at the air-conditioned palaces filled with complimentary women, and burning with a desire to tap the original source of inspiration at its roots, they set out to rediscover the pygmy or the black savage under the solemn pretext of contributing to Science and Knowledge. It was not without an amused anxiety that I asked myself which category of human being I might well represent, as if I could be anything other than that good-natured, continually smiling native whom they saw through the ancient veil of phantasmagoria that had fallen over my country . . . . But how could I resist, how could I not pay hommage to their knowledge, their brilliant learning with its thousands of facts about my barbarism, which had been patiently scrutinized in countless books and which had become the touchstone of the friendship they bore me?

I particularly remember a certain Monsieur Cimetierre, an "Africanist," naturally, who for my benefit undertook to prove that I had not descended from a chicken as, according to him, I was supposed to believe; he also launched into a diatribe against our stupid taboos, vociferously indicting me simply because I had not done honor to the remains of a chicken wing that dripped with his spittle after he had removed the meat from it with timorous pecks, like a bird, and swallowed each mouthful straightaway without chewing (he no longer had any teeth). And late into the night, I was obliged to endure the rasping anteater's laugh, which hideously distorted his face, until his Negress for the night could be heard scratching like a rat outside the building.

One evening as Monsieur Cimetierre continued to bore me with a reading of his notes—I was always subjected to their public debut—it happened that the door, ordinarily graced with a faceless feminine presence, opened upon Anatatchia's self-satisfied smile, which immediately froze on her talcum-powdered white face and then slowly transformed into a mocking grin. Her appearance caused me to forget the humiliating, "oh, master, it's magnificent," with which I customarily punctuated his dull review sessions at the rest house, and I suddenly experienced a violent nausea for everything; she had turned up there, a frightful monument to my lost time, three months of this same smile, and I could now no longer escape the realization that it permeated her being down to that lump of a posterior, furrowed with the same dimples of laughter that gave her rosy-cheeked, worn face an indefinably sad expression of ravaged innocence.

Elbowing my way past Anatatchia, who was half-blocking the doorway, I rushed like a madman into the night.

Eleven

"... I resign! I'm giving notice!" I shouted at Madame Hébrard with a grimace ....

She finally leaned over the counter, on which her breasts were spread out like an enormous octopus slowly suffocating in a cloth sack, and homed in on my lips with one ear, the downy, blotch-covered translucid lobe of which was held taut between her thumb and forefinger.

"... My ... my salary!" I repeated, taking a step forward and holding out my hand.

It was as if I had pulled out a revolver; having finally understood what I was saying, she jerked backward with such alacrity that I, frightened by her bloated, early-morning face, bolted toward the door.

It was nearly the end of the month, a time when she picked quarrels with us as a pretext for cutting our salaries or even depriving us of them altogether. I had never been the victim of this chicanery, not because I exhibited a zeal that immunized me against it, but because in my profession, which consisted exclusively of waiting, it would have been difficult to discover an incriminating dereliction of duty. And Madame Hébrard winced, blanching as the day of reckoning approached, disturbed at the thought that she would have to pay me for the days I had spent daydreaming on the beer-case stage.

Enter Monsieur Cimetierre. Initially exhilarated by the prospect of recouping both my salary and a small profit on his bill, she was soon disabused of her illusions, for with his hermit-like constitution, Monsieur Cimetierre offered few opportunites for her to mitigate the burden of the establishment's general expenses by inflating the cost of his extravagances; besides, he was toothless and an intellectual to boot, never speaking unrestrainedly about anything but his hemorrhoids or his research on the rites and taboos of the local natives.

In the end, Madame Hébrard focused her hostile attentions upon my insignificant person and began to spy on me, to keep me under constant surveillance . . . . And yet I was completely at the mercy of that woman, who could at any moment have discharged me without the slightest ceremony, but she was obsessed with motives, which she probably needed in order to marshal her spitefulness while keeping her employees on a tight leash; she seemed to be unaware of arbitrary dismissals, which were, in her eyes, quite possibly the only imaginable form of injustice. She contented herself with warning me repeatedly, "At the least indiscretion, I'll throw you out on your ass!" This threat had aroused in me an absurd compulsion to persevere, not because I was sufficiently attached to this depressing temporary job to reflect seriously on all the possible indiscretions I might refrain from committing, but perhaps because I did not want to break the habit I had adopted of defying that old woman whose fits of anger I had learned to scorn—it was a tense sort of game that I ultimately won at the end of each month . . . .

And that's how it was; for the first time I was on the verge of losing everything. All that would have been needed was for Monsieur Cimetierre, having awakened early, to hop into the room and rail against my insubordination; then I would have been answerable for my own salary. And it wasn't even because of Anatatchia . . . . To her, with her naiveté of an overly sought-after woman and her dreams of a great romance, my anger must have seemed like the sign of God-knows-what cancerous passion. Until daybreak I had feared she would burst headlong into our hut in the presence of my mother. With her bluntness, her audacity, and her touchiness, Anatatchia indeed belonged to that overpowering race of women whose tyranny quickly transmutes the attention one pays them. I didn't sleep a wink all night, straining to pick up some clue of her intentions with my ears, a seismograph which, subject to the vibrations emanating from my heart, went berserk at the slightest echo of those blunt instruments that are the bared claws of sleep-walkers probing the silence. At a time when the dormant hilltops imparted their incense to a gold and purple sky, I walked out into the early morning dew to take up sentry duty on the outskirts of our compound—I was afraid of Anatatchia's loud and vulgar tone of voice . . . .

An invisible witness, I observed the unobtrusive return of those women who, veiled in their *pagnes,* took advantage of the darkness to wander like nomads through the European section of town. They returned, gliding along the pallid walls of huts, moving from one clump of shadow to another, then disappearing with the creak of a door.

In vain I searched for the elephantine Anatatchia among those unreal silhouettes; she was not there; in his ignorance of local customs, Monsieur Cimetierre had, I thought, perhaps allowed her to sleep late in the European section of town, unless of course her tardiness was due to the invol-

untary prolongation of an overly passionate night that had been inordinately extended . . . . I heard the bugle at the military camp and reflected
that I had already gotten up two hours ago and that in a few moments
Madame Hébrard, coifed in curlers and completely covered with naked
wrinkles beneath her striped dressing gown, was going to open her establishment, cursing as she was greeted by Zebedee, Circumcision Toussaint,
and Saint-Victor the Departed, her trio of assistants whom she affection-
ately, humorously, and rather euphemistically called "wonderful fellows,"
even going so far as to claim maternity for them (which pleased them
enormously), especially when they had emptied the contents of their
hands, tips and all, into her cash drawer, hands which would willingly
have strangled me, for my insouciant manner and irreverent sense of
humor had become pretexts for renewing between us the long-standing
hostility that not so long ago had pitted our tribes against each other.
Breaking off our monolithic solidarity as fellow natives, they had whole-
heartedly sided with the great lady and, in spite of their daily humiliations,
constituted themselves into an ardent band of knights to serve her. These
three stubborn individuals seemed to be waiting for Madame Hébrard to
give them license to unleash the frenzy of wrath that glistened in the angry
glances with which they peppered me from one end of the day to the
other. And now wasn't my previous evening's ill-timed annoyance at
Monsieur Cimetierre, who was probably still asleep at this time of day,
threatening to throw oil onto the fire? What should I do to counter the
impending storm at the Hôtel de France, if not steal a march upon it, hand
in my resignation, quickly collect my salary, and disappear . . . ?

From my vantage point there on the threshold, I kept my eyes riveted
upon the three assistants, whose path was blocked by the counter that
separated us. "And what about me?" continued Madame Hébrard. "A
fool! A damned fool! An idiot! A triple idiot! Ah, yeh got yerself a bed ta lie
in, old girl! Nothin ta say, yer stupid! Cuckolded an' stupid! The El Dorado
that yeh found in the land a Negroes! Well, what yeh got left here, old girl?
All yeh got ta do is go dangle from the rafters at Charenton!* Even if yer a
ol' lady there, yeh won't be insulted by all the chaps what lost their
marbles! Asshole! Yer more of a asshole than a cannibal! Word a honor,
what was yeh thinkin—that the lazy bum sounded reveille fer yer good
looks? Ah, 'scuse me while I laugh! It weren't ta hit yeh? Hit yeh, huh!"
She burst into a peal of hysterical laughter as she opened her cash drawer.
For all that, my attention never wavered from Saint-Victor the Departed,
who seemed the most furious of the three as he prepared to spring, gradually leaning his weight on the counter while the fingers of Circumcision,
who always carried a switchblade knife, drummed on the bar and fixed his

*A well-known insane asylum in Paris. (tr)

crafty eyes on me, watching for any sign of carelessness; as for Zebedee, outstripped by his two colleagues, who were better placed than he was to launch the attack, he appeared to be the most impatient.

Totally unconscious of what was brewing, the corpulent Alsatian woman had opened the cash drawer and was staring at it as she gently caressed and unwrinkled the bills she was bundling together with a rubber band. I had lost all interest in her eyes, and while she continued to fret, those of Circumcision blazed more and more fiercely; his clenched jaw buried between his stevedore's shoulders, he made ready to jump across the counter, behind which his large arms seemed to contract visibly; all that could still be seen were his coarse, spatula-like fingers, which were subject, like lizards in the sun, to sporadic erections. A shiver ran down my back; it was undeniable that the man was trying to reach his switchblade without appearing to do so. Impossible to run away. And yet I had never before been one to stand on dignity. My powerful instinct for survival had always prevailed. But I feared the skill of Circumcision, who could hit any target; would he be aiming for my heart or my eye this time? Run away and expose my shoulder blades to him? The mere thought of a death that strikes you stealthily in the back had transfixed me there on the threshold, from where I could have easily descended into the street; it was just as if I had been driven to the foot of a wall. Here I would have my last chance in the person of Monsieur Cimetierre, for whose arrival I had now devoutly begun to pray. The Business District was calm and deserted; I mused that it was about this time of day when a Syrian merchant had slit the throat of a native assistant who had relieved him of a million francs.* A cold sweat broke out all over my body. I knew the murderous disposition of my older colleague's tribe, and I realized that even by alleging a misunderstanding I would be unable to placate Circumcision. I felt myself growing weaker in the tense, almost unbearable anxiety to which I had been reduced in several minutes by that graying beast, whose hands continued to fascinate me. I remained absolutely motionless, glued to the rough frame of the door and staring intently at the rotating movements of Circumcision's powerful torso; he was now stretched across the counter, having succeeded in sliding his large arms back beneath his chest and behind the counter, where they were lurking in wait for a propitious moment in which to throw his knife at me in a flash.

How long did we remain in that position? I was beginning to feel a tingling in my legs and the onset of a cramp; my vision clouded over, and I vacillated between believing that Circumcision had slid his hand beneath the counter and that he had not . . . . The sound of several cars could be heard as they were being driven out of their garages. The Business District

---

*In francophone Africa, fifty francs CFA are equivalent to one French franc. (tr)

was becoming animated. I was no longer afraid, perhaps because I credited Circumcision with the common sense that would oblige him to postpone his heinous crime now that my cries might attract a crowd. I became bold to the point of being the first to smile at my adversaries, but contrary to my expectation, the situation grew worse; I hadn't seen anything, but above my head I heard the drumming of a woodpecker at the very moment when I glimpsed the fleeting gleam of a knife blade emerging from beneath the counter and Circumcision charging me with a series of gutteral grunts. What happened? I saw him on the ground and me kicking him furiously; then I felt myself being grabbed around the waist by his confederates. They would have hacked me to pieces if my cries for help, in conjunction with those of Madame Hébrard, had not brought her husband rushing into the shop in his pyjamas. The European had been waiting a long time for his chance, and he thought it presented a perfect opportunity to revive the hallowed tradition of the cudgel. He armed himself with a bottle, which he immediately discarded after weighing it carefully; then, seizing the thick rubber tube with heavy lead rings that was used for siphoning the red wine, he began to hit us with all his might, fiendishly, his face flushed, his mouth foaming. We fled to the four corners of the bar, where he pursued us, brandishing his hose and whirling it in the air like a lasso before smacking it down on our backs. Lacking the patience to wait for us to crawl out from beneath the counter, where we had dived helter-skelter to find some sort of refuge, he leaped on top of it and struck us a number of blows until we were forced to leave our derisory shelter. A moment later he landed near the door, cutting off our retreat, and there he stood breathless, bent over, his legs spread, his minuscule foreskin dangling frugally in the slit on the front of his pyjama bottoms, his teeth bared, and his hair pointing in all directions as he challenged us to attack.

"Come on, sons of bitches! You're afraid, eh? What are you waiting for, eh, you bushy-tailed monkeys! Come closer! Do come closer! The door is wide open. What's holding you back? Ah! That's better! You're not trying to be smart any more; you're not shouting any more . . . ."

"Calm yourself; you want to go to France," I repeated to myself like an incantatory charm to exorcise the anger that smoldered in my every limb and goaded me on.

He screamed for a long time, calling us "Communist bastards" and shouting at his wife to "shut up"; to my great relief, he finally released his hold on the impromptu club and pounced on the cash drawer, which he somehow succeeded in separating from his wife. He removed the rubberband from a wad of bills in order to pay me and rid himself of the black sheep . . . .

In a trance, I walked out into the street.

Twelve

"Still nothing!" the native employee told me with a harsh sigh as his bison-like shadow sauntered back and forth behind the bars of the post-office window. Exasperated with giving me the same sempiternal reply, the irascible brute was beginning to take a dislike to me. His colleagues turned around apprehensively at his outburst of grumbling, which obliged me to affect all sorts of studiedly self-confident gestures to compose myself as I backed away from the counter with a dignified, indifferent air that I immediately lost when I reached the street and collapsed onto the same old stone marker, where I felt my reason being overcome by fear and despair. How many times had I sat this way on the edge of the road in all sorts of weather, hearing nothing, seeing nothing, and repeating to myself, "they don't want to send me to France." And each day was a repetition of the preceding one: as soon as I awoke, I ran to the European section of town, animated by my nocturnal imaginings that revolved around the letter I was expecting. The saffron-yellow roof of the post office loomed up; it hit me square in the chest with the force of a battering ram. It was then that confusion overwhelmed me; breathless, dazed, and bathed in sweat, I no longer knew if I had come here of my own accord or if someone had summoned me. Without stifling my euphoria, this disordered state of mind prevented me from distinguishing clearly between the real and the imaginary, so strong was the intensity of the delusive intuition that drove me to the post office even after seven months of administrative silence . . . . On that day I could not make up my mind to face the native employee. From the veranda I was repulsed by the enormous conical wart that stood vigil in the layer of black fat on his neck. I rushed quickly down the stairs at precisely the moment when he, having surmised my presence, turned around on his high stool. I waited until nightfall to follow him, hoping he would talk about the letter during the course of his solitary walk when, in a delirium of anger, he began to trumpet a bizarre monologue, attacking

77

nearby shrubbery and elusive fireflies with powerful kicks of his foot. We made the round of every hovel in the native section of town, I following him like an old Chinese woman in pursuit of her husband and occasionally spying on him from outside through lighted cracks in the mud-and-wattle walls. I left him when he became completely drunk and, to the hypocritical indignation of the women, removed his pants to put them on the top of his head.

I relapsed into boredom, passing my days at home in the contemplation of spiders and cockroaches winding their way through stalactites of soot . . . .

I was good for nothing, and people made me aware of it in a flattering manner. While paying homage to my vast learning, they scoffed at my eternal vacation as a great man without a job. "You're only fit for books!" exclaimed my mother, who had forbidden me access to her little bamboo cabin, concealed behind our hut and lying on the other side of a cocoa planting, a pestiferous stream, and a cassava field; it lay on the outskirts of the forest, and she wended her way there every morning to preside over the clandestine distillation of the corn alcohol that would enable me to pay for my trip to France. In trying to help her, I had only succeeded in tipping over the still and reducing to nought the three-week fermentation of a hundred kilos of fresh corn sprouts, the slow germination of which it had been my task to supervise.

I loitered about in the noxious dust of the Business District, where people greeted me with mockingly exaggerated doffs of the hat; I then wandered over to the courthouse and returned by way of the post office and the public school, which reverberated with the cries of youngsters being beaten and calling for their mothers all day long . . . . That was where the native teachers gave free rein to their sadism. The hospital stood gaping on the other side of the playground, and from time to time one saw a child run into it, streaming with blood and emitting a continuous, high-pitched wail. The child cried there for a long time and even more afterward; furious at having been obliged to leave the shade of the veranda, where he spent his days launching obscene comments in the direction of passersby, the male nurse doused the wound with iodine before angrily bandaging the child's head in haste, so he himself could hurry back to the veranda . . . . I finally returned to the market place, where the native merchants—reeking strongly of naphthalene, gasoline, spices, and medicines (each retailer exuding the odors of his own shop)—welcomed me with broad smiles, the keys to the cash box, which had previously been double-locked in anticipation, having been buried in the depths of their pockets . . . . They salaamed effusively, their evasive expressions and heavy, damp, furtive handshakes a prelude to their humble request that I cast an eye—"oh, just a little glance, nothing at all really"—over their papers, all of which enabled them to obtain for nothing what amounted to a real balancing of the books.

These merchants were distributed among three immense sheds. There they set up their stalls, in which phonographs played cacophonously throughout the day; also, there was always a bed cleverly concealed behind their display of merchandise. It was here that they obliged the impecunious women of the market to repay them in kind—girls from the public school, the nun's pupils on recess, and the wives of civil servants for the most part, the latter especially toward the end of the month. I also went there to write an endless stream of letters; to compensate me for my pains, they entreated me to add, "this letter was written for me, whose ignorance is, alas, quite well known to you, by Monsieur Barnabas, our Savior who was so unjustly expelled from the Seminary . . . ."

I then returned to the street and walked briskly down it, delirious in the childish joy of knowing that I was useful, indispensible. I would have persisted in this illusion, if I had not ventured along the path to the backwater one evening at a time when the flash of fireflies riddles the fog and shadow like a silent display of fireworks, and the women, a utensil under the arm, go to perform their final ablutions, swaying languidly to the rhythm of a call-and-response refrain but invariably ready to dissolve into a violent peal of laughter announcing the mutual confession of indiscretions.

I was still there on the edge of the path, incredulous at the remarks I was hearing when Anatatchia's laugh (I had avoided her since our last encounter at the rest house) suddenly caused me to straighten up, for her companions had fallen silent to listen to her.

"Him! Ha! Ha! Don't make me laugh! God the Father, the Holy Trinity, and all the Saints can bear me witness that it was something to see. Ai-yee, mama mia! The seminary, that'll preserve your little man for you! Only, why . . . as for me, it was out of curiosity that I let him try me on, a passing fancy eh, but him, the rogue, he wants to move in like as if he'd bought my little box!"

A chorus of women replied, each having been titillated at the same moment and in the same spot. ". . . And yet that's not what people would suspect when they see his mug of a stray foreigner who wants to do poo-poo."

"Don't trust appearances! I know my little man, like I'm telling you. Look, we could've been happy, the two of us; a woman, she knows how to find her man quickly enough. Only, why . . . him, he has delusions of grandeur, like all those men who've been deprived of women for too long; it goes to their heads. Besides, it's not with me, who don't give a damn about white folks, that a stone-broke nigger is going to try and act smart. With somebody else maybe, but I tells him to go fuck himself! I couldn't stand his questions no longer . . . ."

"Which ones?"

"Out with it!"

A weak volley of laughter.

". . . Even if it was worse than what you confessed to Father L——. . . ."

A moment of silence; then laughter broke out a second time, as if it were merely the echo of the first outburst.

"Ai-yee, my beloved dead! Every time I leave that place, I'm trembling, and in spite of the benediction, the absolution, and the rosary of penitence, I get a prickly feeling all over on account of those questions he throws into my soul like fish hooks to catch my sins . . . !"

"How can he, who's a man of God, know all that?"

"Ha! Ha! Ha! Don't make me laugh! Him! But who ever told you he didn't enjoy life before? It's not virgins they're going to send over here to probe so good into those sweet delicacies that spice and aggravate the sin of the thing . . . ."

"She's right!"

"Yes, as for me, I have a funny feeling when he starts to . . . ."

"You do? But so do I, Jesus-Mary-and-Joseph! One time even, when it took hold of him like that, like a laxative, I asked myself if it weren't the devil in person that the Good Lord had sent to do a bit of housecleaning in my soul! He wouldn't stop; I was sweating all over, and I says to myself how this fellow knows every nook and cranny in hell!"

"Him? Ha! Ha! Ha! Don't make me laugh! Ain't it true he was first a good little French soldier? And after all, ain't it God who gave us the thing . . . ."

"She's right!"

"Ha! Ha! Ha! Don't make me laugh, oh, you who talk as if the little box weren't the same for everyone, and in the same place too!"

"No argument there! You can't say that's not the Good Lord's truth!"

"She's right, by the Holy Apostles! And I know something about it! That's the reason I almost been killed; oh, I would have been with my beloved dead for a long time now! One evening there's my husband getting up quietly after . . . instead of beginning to snore right away like he always done during the ten years we been married. At first I didn't understand nothing about what was happening to him; he looked at me, and then he just raises the wick of the lamp again, so he can pound on me all night long with a slat from the bed. Ah, my beloved dead! And why? So I can tell him the name of my lover—the white man who taught me all that! 'There's a white man behind it, and God sees him!' he cried, 'and I won't stop until you tell me his name! You done it with me like I never thought about; you did it too complicated for us niggers! Where you been?' and me, I got nothing to say; for me, it had become like a long story he couldn't ever have understood. I believe the Good Lord, who's just and who sees everything, is storing me up a martyr's crown for that day . . . ."

"Oh! Lord! What we got to hear! As many as we is, we all going to hell, and with our asses in the air, like I'm telling you, now that poor black ladies is only going to confession to learn the tricks of the devil!"

"Is it our fault? You got to admit that religion don't have much of a chance with poor black ladies!"

"God, as for Him, He knows religion's got a chance, because Barnabas, he never become a priest!"

"Why not? He's tall, flabby, and not much fun; the frock would'a looked very good on him . . . . In my opinion, he would'a made a good priest."

"Him?" interjected Anatatchia with a cry that pierced me to the core. "The scourge of the good sisters, you mean!"

They again burst into laughter and intoned the credo that they sang good-naturedly in bad Latin every morning in the prayer house, where the priest's local auxiliary ludicrously fulfilled the duties of his office. He was a lusty, untutored fellow who, like many idiots, was endowed with an excellent memory that permitted him to pretend he was reading the Scriptures, which he actually was reciting despite the fact that his nose was buried in a Petit Larousse Illustré, the most voluminous tome he could find in the town's only library.

The women remained silent. Several splashes bored through the silence; then, the sound of hands shoveling water and the plash of bathing could be heard . . . .

"And now, what's his intentions?"

"Who . . .? Ah, our would-be priest! Intentions, my God! That's all he's got! Seems he wants to go to the white man's country, to France . . . ."

"To France? Why France? Is he tired of poor black ladies?"

"I think there's a bit of that in it, but he can't admit it . . . . His pet notion, it's to go to school over there and become somebody!"

"Ah . . . ."

"But I who know him can tell you, and the Virgin is my witness, that this snotty-nosed brat who sneers at everyone will never amount to much. Just wait, and you'll see him among Olinga's prisoners one of these days! A good for nothing, I tell you, except when he is making love!"

They laughed.

"Poor fellow! I feel sorry for him . . . ."

"I never saw anyone who lets people pull the wool over his eyes like that; it's a fact that if my little Ambroise ever became like him, I'd kill him first and then me . . . ."

"What good does it really do him to have been at school if he ain't even shrewd enough to see that nobody gives a damn about him? Ain't it sad to see a chap who speaks French better than anyone in the neighborhood just wandering all over the place like a donkey who got no master and works for just anybody!"

"I see you don't know him very well! Ha! Ha! Ha! Don't make me laugh! If you only knew! Well then, this chap, I never heard him say, 'so-and-so is somebody!' For him, everyone is less than nothing, an asshole, eh! A woman is just good for fucking, if that! And the bastard, he who was so well preserved in the seminary, he did it to me like breaking a hard-boiled egg; all I had to do was get on with it, and even after he closed his eyes to make as if he was feeling good, you didn't dare look too closely. God knows I've had a few men in my time, but one like him I never seen before! Well then, you can say anything you want, but as for me, I got my own little theory about him—nothing but a madman, I tell you!"

"Jesus-Mary-and-Joseph! Ain't it what I always thought!"

"Me too, by the Holy Apostles!"

"As for me, it don't surprise me; seems his father . . . ."

I couldn't bear to listen any longer and sneaked away.

Thirteen

In the bus that was going to take me to Y——, I rested my head in the palm of my hand and tried to think as a way of beguiling my impatience to see us underway.

It was early in the morning; they left that early so as to arrive in the capital before the heat and mushrooming dust clouds of noon. The marketplace served as a loading dock, and although it was ordinarily quite calm and deserted at this time of day, it had now come to life with an unusual bustle of activity. Flanked by family or friends and struggling under the burden of their loads, late-arriving travelers emerged from the shadows and dashed toward the only open door of the bus, where the "Ticket-Collector," a thirty-odd-year-old Hercules whose wife (he was wearing a wedding band) had clumsily embroidered his function with white thread on the jacket of a red suit he had had made for himself, kept driving them back with kicks and shoves as he roared at them to give him some breathing room; he opened the double-ended sack that he carried on a shoulder-strap and buried in it the money which he seized as it was handed to him in a frenzy, issuing in exchange a little pink ticket that permitted one to dart inside the wide-bodied Berliet, of which the proud but still absent owner was a young Greek who enjoyed an absolute monopoly on the exploitation of passenger traffic along this 250-kilometer stretch of road.

The hubbub of departure took place under the sporadic illumination of a native policeman's flashlights, which would shine upon some savagely scarified, folkloric, sleep-swollen face that jerked backward and kept blinking like an old nag suffering from toothache and refusing its oats, or they would shoot out a beam, like that of a doctor's headlamp probing straight to the uvula of a palate yawning with drowsiness and resembling the wide-open gullet of some famished or well-fed saurian on the beach

. . . .

83

The crowd grew larger around the enormous vehicle as if it were the providential corpse of an elephant that villagers were besieging to still their insatiable longing for meat. It was a heterogeneous crowd: Hausas parading about in their shimmering gandouras and weighed down by their traveling bazaars temporarily rolled inside mats from which dangled a classic enamel coffee pot filled with the purifactory water that was indispensible for worshipping Allah; ludicrous, bewildered, mostly Catholic peasants, their dirty, open collars encumbered with a necktie, a scapulary, a rosary, and a *gris-gris* that hung from a string. These peasants reeked of the peanut sauce they had eaten in the hope of shielding themselves from any temptation to taste the contemptible dishes of contemptible city-dwellers. There were also plump traders, clasping their snakeskin briefcases under their arms and remaining stationary to demonstrate their importance; minor civil servants wearing suits patched with pretentious badges and angrily brandishing their travel orders as they threatened to file an official complaint; native soldiers jostling their way past everyone else to take inside seats, where they arranged their canteens and haversacks with as much care as if they were bedding down a pair of twins . . . . And then there was the brouhaha in front of the door, where chattering women wrapped in interminably voluminous *pagnes* or decked out in European clothes (some of them even daring to prefer the impermanent artificial red, which performed double duty on their thick lips, to the natural and quite tenacious tint that the Good Lord had pasted on them for life) calmly endured the annoyance inflicted upon them by the whining products of their fertility—brats, spoiled for the most part and already devouring, by themselves, a chicken leg or a large piece of meat that would have more than satisfied the hunger of an adult at this hour of the day. Then too, there were the animals: mangy, flea-ridden dogs and irascible sheep destined as bribes for some European or native dignitary from whom their owners expected to solicit a favor . . . .

The bus was filled up with all these people, who remained indifferent to the brutality and vulgarity of the "Ticket-Collector" bobbing about in the doorway and nervously swiveling his game-pouch in all directions as he switched it from one side to the other during his hand-to-hand combats with the passengers, whom he kept at bay by kicking them repeatedly or, if necessary, by grabbing them around the neck. Finally, he turned around, calculated the number of remaining seats, filled them, and then savagely closed the doors, to the despair of the non-elect, who burst into insults and curses, menacing "Cerdan" (the ticket-collector's unlikely surname) with fists and clenched teeth as he took up a position behind the windshield and replied to them tit for tat. Exhausted, he went over and collapsed into the driver's seat, but not before dusting it first with a red-embroidered white handkerchief, which he then slipped into the little pocket on his jacket, making certain that it protruded slightly and regarding it with a brief, self-satisfied glance that precipitated a cascade of ripples among the folds of his chin.

On the roof, two "motor-boys" were moving about, arranging the animals and the luggage they had carried on the top of their heads or draped across their shoulders as they mounted the little metal ladder affixed to the back of the bus. It was up there that they habitually traveled and passed their time, and that was one of the reasons why the natives, who in those days paid for this illusory driving school with their labors, often squandered a good part of their lives in a vain attempt to obtain their licenses.

I was huddled beside the window next to a native civil servant, a plain male nurse who sported a garnet-colored *kepi* with three gold stripes of a captain-surgeon in the colonial expeditionary force! Surrounded by his four wives, who varied considerably in age, he derived a great deal of satisfaction from it. His two oldest wives were dressed in European clothes and sat facing us, each with her own three- or four-year-old offspring, both of whom had been endowed with the same flat nose that was barely discernible in the ape-like profile of the father. He was a little, fifty-year-old man who had kept everything at his side, including, on his right, an obviously pregnant, sixteen- or seventeen-year-old fourth wife. In the aisle, several other twelve- to fourteen-year-old children displayed the same nose as the younger ones across from us.

I dared not turn around for fear of encountering a familiar face; I no longer felt I had the patience to endure its hypocritical amiability. I was afraid of some uncontrollable impulse on my part . . . . I was glued to the window, which clouded over with my breath; everything inside the bus— the lights, the silhouettes—suffused into the unreal. I congratulated myself on the long-awaited trip that I was finally about to undertake. I held in my hands the chance to become capable of humiliating those who had all too quickly viewed my temporary setbacks as a vindication of their gloomy prophecies during those difficult times when I, possessing neither fortune nor benefactor, was painfully seeking my way. At that thought, I felt myself fill with boldness to wrest a fellowship from the Government to study in France—a fellowship that all by itself had the capacity to sanctify you in a country where people worshipped anyone blessed with the rare privilege of departing to receive an education in France. I experienced something like a weekend of thought . . . but the Greek, the owner of the bus, had still not arrived.

The passengers began to grow impatient; as they overcame their irritation, a galley slave's solidarity arose among them and encouraged good neighborly relations to the detriment of "Cerdan," who was tallying his receipts as he lounged in his boss' seat. He no longer responded or shot back sarcastic insults in the midst of all these ill-humored people, who seemed ready to avenge themselves inside the bus for the brutalities to which they had remained indifferent as long as they had not yet acquired the little pink ticket, which they now, with a sudden start, fingered in its place of security behind an ear, between two breasts, in the internal or external band of a hat, on the inside of a jacket, or between a wedding ring and a ring finger, assuring themselves of its presence there before admonishing the ticket-collector to go in search of his accursed boss, with whom they were beginning to suspect him of having contrived the most devious schemes. In the throes of a sudden and possibly sham rage that subsequently proved difficult for others to calm, an angry passenger arose periodically from his seat to go and "punch him in the face." As far as the ticket-collector was concerned, he hardly gave the impression of wanting to defend himself; he shriveled humbly into his boss' seat, huddled over his pouch and clutching it tightly against his chest as he swept the entire scene with the frightened look of a dog being threatened with a stick. In the end, he tried to pass himself off as the pathetic victim of a "vile profession," in which he incurred the risk of making enemies—"fortunately for me I don't have any ambitions to run in the next election"—but which he found himself obliged to continue practicing in order to feed his family, for whom he was, "by the will of God," the sole support, his grandmother being afflicted, moreover, with leprosy and paralysis . . . .

And although he recited this mitigating story like a bad actor, it nevertheless obtained the intended success, for in the inmost recesses of their hearts, the passengers had become convinced that the man's boss was to blame for everything. Suddenly someone cried out, "At last! There he is! He's not in much of a hurry; he doesn't give a damn about us!" Sure enough, Monsieur Stephinades could be seen approaching with his shirt sleeves rolled up. No one having replied to the greeting of the white man, who had in the meantime seated himself behind the steering wheel, we drove off in a hostile silence.

We had been underway for several hours; the morning acquired definition as it wore on . . . . We passed through village after village, all of them the same with their double row of huts scattered along either side of the road, their goats in stampede, their children testing their prowess against the speed of the bus, their groups of men issuing from a makeshift chapel in *pagnes* that were majestically draped over their shoulders like Roman togas, their women pausing for an instant to look at us before emptying a basket of garbage or setting down a water-filled recepticle balanced on top of their heads.

The bus stopped from time to time, whenever one of the passengers addressed an onomatopoeia or a guttural cry to the Greek as an indication of his intention to get off or else hurriedly left his seat and began banging insistently on the door with his fist. If he spoke pidgin, he shouted, "Wai-ait! Matoa wait!"* We followed him with our eyes as long as he continued sending us broad, indecipherable semaphore signals by waving his arms and legs in a frenzied dance, for which the only rhythm was provided by the throbbing of our diesel engine . . . .

Wearying of this endlessly recurrent spectacle, I had allowed myself to fall into a hypnotic daze when a violent slap suddenly rocked my shoulder and sent an electrical impulse shooting to the medulla. It was Bendjanga-Boy, the seller of contaminated shrimp, who had materialized there like a ghost in a nightmare, having cleared a spot for himself in the aisle between the seats by a skillful deployment of his elbows. He was one of those spiteful beings whom I did not want to see again before my triumphant return. Seeing him there, jovial, self-satisfied, fat, with his rat's face and his Sunday suit, carrying a briefcase that (to judge by the vigor with which he clutched it to his side) was of utmost importance, swaying comically and stretching out his free hand to grope for a point of support which could only be the shoulder of a sullen, frowning woman whom he dared not touch, I had the impression of suffocating and felt myself grow tense, ready to snap at someone . . . .

"What the hell are you doing here, you of all people?" he exclaimed in a disdainful tone of voice—his "you" pierced me like a dart. I looked at him, preparing to smash my head into those rotten teeth that were mocking me. Perhaps because he had a somber premonition of my intentions, he stopped laughing and smiled at me, this time with an air of complicity, as he said, "It's a pleasure to meet an old pal in these parts! I left L—— three days ago to bring a taste of the sea to these folks, who usually gorge themselves on nothing but roots and leaves, just like the pygmies; no question about it—that's why they're such assholes."

The local people in the bus betrayed themselves by taking offense at his remarks. After an exchange of taunts had provoked the indignation of some and elicited the joy of others, the protagonists would have come to blows if the Greek hadn't slammed on the brakes, threatening to kick us all off and give us our money back.

"It's all right! It's all right!" said Bendjanga-Boy, rearranging the knot in his necktie. "This country is all screwed up! You can't even joke around any more, like our ancestors used to do, without getting into trouble!" Then, continuing to cast himself in the hero's role, he proceeded, "how do you know that I'm actually thinking what I'm saying? Don't we all pay taxes? Well then, and why did I come out this way, if it wasn't because an idea had occurred to me in town, out of the blue, that I really ought to bring some seafood to my brothers, folks who don't get down to the sea as

---

*"Stop, automobile, stop!" in pidgin.

much as I do, and I brought them, Good Lord, I brought them a hundred kilos of shrimp, and they paid me for them, not with the cash for the taxes, which they take like kola nuts, without even thinking about it, from a basket hanging on a nail next to the door, but with the stuff they bury under their beds where they make love; and all that, don't it show that I was a brother and that my shrimps made them happy . . . ? Well then, how can anyone believe what I think I've only said jokingly . . . ."

In any case, silence had fallen in the bus, and, changing the topic of conversation, Bendjanga-Boy asked me where I was going, and what I was planning to do in the capital, and if I was leaving for France "on the sly" as a "little bird had told him." There was a movement in my direction; the male nurse turned toward me, looking at me as if he were discovering my presence for the first time.

Bendjanga-Boy continued, "I know what the others been saying to you, but I can tell you plainly, like a little brother whom I love from the bottom of my heart, that you're going to be making a mistake! Eh, what! Who do you know over there? A man, it don't take long for a man to fall sick; well then, who'll take care of you, tell me that? And when you want to talk to somebody, who're you going to find? Who'll understand you over there . . . ? Our ancestors, they used to say, 'you can tell the size of an elephant by the size of his turds,' well then, just look around this country—you ever eat at the same table as a European? Well then, you think he's going to invite you to dinner over there in his country? Sure, you're smarter than I am, and you know damned well that when I needed a little paperwork, it was you who prepared it for me out of the goodness of your heart . . . ."

That generous heart contracted abruptly.

"God knows if I got a few pennies!" He patted his briefcase. "What am I going to do with all this money which my little affairs with shrimp have brought in for me. Well then, I says to myself, Bendjanga-Boy, you're going to die without ever experiencing life . . . . When they nail the last board over your coffin, what's going to happen to all your coins, and you without even a single wife? You've got to take a little jaunt to the big city, I said to myself; up there it seems that . . . ."

He posed his fat, ring-laden forefinger on his lips, rolled his eyes from left to right, and whispered loudly to me, "I'll tell you, nobody but you alone; it's a state secret . . . ."

He then proceeded in a normal tone of voice. "Barnabas, those who told you that you ought to go over there, they're not your friends . . . ! We'd make a fantastic team, the two of us, and it's me who's telling you!" He patted his briefcase again. "What with all you know, we could become kings of the shrimp trade in this country . . . !"

Then the woman, whose shoulder Bendjanga-Boy had dared not

touch, suddenly extricated herself from her seat, rushed over to me, and in full view of everyone pressed a thousand-franc note into my hand; then, standing back to get a better view of me, she peppered my face with a volley of brackish saliva that had been discolored by the quid of tobacco swelling in her scarified cheek (it was her way of blessing me); then she cried, "Go ahead, my child, go to their country, become a Commandant, a Commissa,* marry one of their women; that'll change a lot of things for us in this country! Just don't listen to this snake . . . !" She broke into a nervous laugh that dilated the veins in her neck, treated an incredulous Bendjanga-Boy to a disdainful sweeping glance, and returned to her seat.

"Ah, this is the happiest day of my life," exclaimed my neighbor, the male nurse, who removed his *kepi,* groped about the inside of his jacket, and extracted two one-thousand-franc notes. "God be with you!" he continued, pointing to the Greek with the tip of his chin. Only at that moment did I realize that his ears were sticking out. In tones of mystical illumination, my neighbor thundered, "Come back and save us like Moses saved the children of Israel from the bondage of Egypt!" His words were greeted with a murmur of approval.

First it was the turn of the peasants, then that of the soldiers, who stood at attention while presenting me with their five-hundred-franc notes, which I quickly put into my pocket. That was the signal for a general onslaught; passengers from the back of the bus rushed forward in waves, pushing and shoving each other in their enthusiasm to bring me their money; I no longer had time to stuff it into my pockets, and since both my hands and the lap between my tightly-pressed thighs were overflowing with it, someone offered me a broad-brimmed hat . . . . The Greek, flushed with anger, once again slammed on the brakes. The passengers were hurled violently against each other, and they began to scream. They demonstrated, held a parley, and finally it was the male nurse who, seconded by one of the soldiers and after having retrieved his *kepi,* explained to the Greek that "the Country was taking leave of this young man"—he pointed to me with his finger—that "God had designated us to help send him to study in France," and that "a special chartered plane" was waiting for me that afternoon. He turned around and winked at me. The Greek, in whose eyes I saw myself growing in stature, apologized and even executed something like a salute by passing his forefinger above his ear before settling into his seat again and driving off . . . .

I sat there embarrassed and puzzled, not knowing what to say, not daring to protest, to deliver myself from the notoriety which had been invested in me and which was now being trumpeted by the exuberant male nurse, who had suddenly been transformed into a herald whose

---

*Commissaire de police (police chief).

shouts attracted the passengers being loaded at the back of the bus, from where they staggered forward to spit profusely in my face at the price of a coin or a wrinkled bill that they threw into the hat like Pharisees.

"Come say your goodbye to this son of our country, this child whom God has chosen to go study in the white man's country, from where he'll come back to save us, to save Africa!" And he babbled on without pausing, all the while casting furious glances at Bendjanga-Boy, who finally, at the 232-kilometer mark, quit staring obstinately at the passing countryside. To make peace with the other passengers and not to be remiss on his own account, he decided to open his briefcase.

"It always brought me luck to do what everyone else was doing!" he said as he pulled out a thousand-franc note.

"It's about time!" someone commented.

"Indeed!" observed Bendjanga-Boy as he looked at the speaker with astonishment and then, dissimulating his thoughts, added, "I believe everything I was taught by the holy and apostolic Roman Catholic Church, and there's not another person like me for knowing the story of the Good Samaritan, which is a story that's always brought me luck, the very one they were always asking me about on the examinations for my baptism, my first communion, and my confirmation, which I always passed without lifting a finger! No question about it, I was born under the sign of that story . . . !" And gripping the bill in his hand, which he swung rapturously above his head, he released it into my hat with an animal-like cry. The passengers applauded . . . .

In this overheated atmosphere we arrived at Y——, and before I could launch into lavish expressions of gratitude, I was once again embraced, poked, congratulated, shaken, and jostled about, much to the amazement of bystanders in the city . . . . But I was soon alone once more, after a policeman arrived on the scene and ordered us to "get moving . . . ."

Fourteen

With all that money bulging in my pockets, I inclined toward optimism, but it was a tense, restrained optimism tainted by a sudden fear inspired in me by my fellow countrymen, who had become like strangers seemingly consumed with a cold-blooded determination to commit some felony. I was constantly turning around, and I gave a start from time to time, whenever I had the impression that someone was following me or had brushed past me too closely. Stooped like a hunchback by my suspicions and convulsed with a groundless rage, I abandoned the sidewalk, which was overflowing at that hour of the day with a seething flood of naked feet and incredible worn-out shoes that pounded the burning, cracked, and fissured asphalt in the savage gallop of stampeding solipeds as the daily flood of natives, workers, clerks, civil servants, children, idlers, and delinquents ebbed and flowed between the European section of town and the black neighborhood, which could be divined in the distance by virtue of the stagnant, mushroom-shaped cloud of dust and smoke, speckled with thousands of slowly revolving black spots the size of ebony soup plates—hawks, vultures, and buzzards intermingling in congealed flight, apparently trapped in the viscous eddies of a resinous ocean.

Once again I found myself forsaken, crushed by the heat, standing at a crossroads. In front of me, houses made entirely of windows rose in unbroken tiers, eclipsing the horizon as they dozed beneath a foliage of the gilded, purified, copper-tinted yellow that old tobacco leaves eventually acquire. The stiffness of these somnolent, lifeless houses reminded one of gigantic tombs in a necropolis that had been restored, American-style, around a discolored little obelisk shrouded in smoke by a solitary tired locomotive idling along roundhouse tracks that were separated from the street by a hedge of stunted hibiscus bushes on which five or six ragged railway workers were urinating as they chatted noisily among themselves.

I raised myself on my toes and, shading my eyes with one hand, scrutinized that indefinable something in this steam-bath atmosphere to find some clue that might have indicated the seat of Government to me.

"We're not in the provinces, the bush where everyone thinks it's so simple that all you got to do is 'put your foot on the road,' set your sails, and hop out right in front of your door! And I even thought you were going to bring me luck . . . ."

At first I had jumped when I saw the shadow dissolve as it spread over my own like a spot of dirty fuel oil. It was only Bendjanga-Boy. He had just loomed up behind me, wrapped in the faint tannery odor that emanated from the boa-skin briefcase he was clutching under his arm. He too exerted himself to locate a place he wanted to find, raising himself ponderously on the tips of his canvas shoes as his grotesquely protruding belly swung back and forth like that of a five-month pregnant woman; he was completely absorbed, his eyebrows furrowed, his bent forefinger resting on his lips.

"Even if the most difficult part is about to begin," he mumbled to me, casting a sidewise glance in my direction, "got to shift for one's self, can't ask for directions; people could lure us somewhere and then slit our throats; got to go door to door, that's all!"

He staggered slightly as he fell back on his heels, paused, and hesitated momentarily with a crafty look in his eye before taking out an interminable handkerchief, which was actually an old scarf adorned with obscene pictures, and trying to mop himself off with it.

"Nothing but a flag," he said, discouraged, as he raised his rapidly blinking little porcine eyes toward me with a look of disillusionment.

"What, that?" I asked, disdainfully pointing to his swollen pocket.

"No, no, over there!" he replied with bad grace, raising a bare, sweat-beaded arm and aiming it above his head.

I then made out something that could just as easily not have been a banner waving, miniscule, in front of us at the far end of a block of houses, where it was obscured in a cloud of dust undoubtedly raised by phantom cars driving on the other side of the city and emitting sounds we might perhaps have heard in muffled form, despite the distance and the tons of stone and cement that separated us from them, if the little locomotive opposite us had not shaken heaven and earth with an infernal screaching of metal. Smitten with a veritable frenzy of oneiric reflections, Bendjanga-Boy was shouting at the top of his voice amid this bedlam and didn't stop until we both jumped into the air, our ears harpooned by the piercing wail of the whistle, which the engineer of the misbegotten little train took pleasure in blowing at any moment, perhaps to communicate in his own way with a wife or a mistress who, each time, experiences raptures of happiness somewhere in the native section of the city . . . .

"A fine profession!" exclaimed Bendjanga-Boy, grabbing me by the elbow . . . .

Surprised and intrigued, I didn't follow him immediately and asked myself what had earned me the affected company of Bendjanga-Boy, for I didn't figure among his friends; he had never even taken the trouble to escort me to the rectangle of rotten planks that served in lieu of a door to his shack, contenting himself to open the latch with a kick after having succeeded in inveigling me to examine his accounts for nothing. Did he want to recover the thousand-franc note he had only agreed to give me under the threat of being flayed alive on the bus? To lend him a helping hand, I questioned him about the matter without beating around the bush, all the while burrowing in my pockets.

"How can you . . . Good Lord! I'm just keeping you company . . . but how, God all . . . ," he stammered offended, his chest swelling in a single motion and remaining frozen in place as if it were about to bust.

I suppressed an urge to laugh. I was no longer on this earth; I must be encountering Bendjanga-Boy on some other planet. His generosity could only portend some favor he wanted to ask of me. I resigned myself to waiting. We moved forward, one behind the other, in silence. We stopped again at the foot of a light pole that, during the night, presumably illuminated the cut-throat latrines along the old wall surrounding an immense garage; attracted by the rustling of a remarkably green foliage at this point, we had imprudently plunged into a shortcut to reach the seat of Government by aiming for the flag, or what was supposed to be a flag, disappearing and reappearing like a kite above the palm trees in the dusty atmosphere.

After casting a brief glance to the left and to the right and then spitting between his legs, Bendjanga-Boy unbuttoned his pants. I had time neither to turn around nor to spit and thereby ward off the evil eye by purifying myself; the bad-luck curse as they call it in the village immediately took possession of my being, because I had glimpsed something as maleficent as the rare multi-colored lizard in the wet hammocks—the sexual organ of one of my elders!

At least that is the mystico-superstitious explanation to which I eventually had recourse when my star pupil's logic proved incapable of rationally justifying the intransigence that I was about to confront on the part of Monsieur Dansette. People had told me many good things about him. He was one of those grand gentlemen whose sonorous-sounding titles signified—above all and especially for me—an independence of mind, an integrity, an intelligence, and a spirit of generosity that one could not seriously call into question. Now that I regularly run into people whose stupidity, meanness, and fanaticism clash violently with their station in life, I long ago exculpated the wrinkled old penis of Bendjanga-Boy, who in fact had nothing at all to do with Monsieur Dansette's bovine persistence in desiring to enroll me at all costs in a local trade school.

"Believe me, it would be in your best interest!"

"Monsieur," I replied in desperation, "perhaps I didn't express myself clearly, but I want to go to France; that's all I live for!"

"I understand! I understand, my poor friend! France! It's the most beautiful country in the world and . . . ."

"That's just the reason why I . . . ."

"But you've got to be realistic, see! What'll you do there? And for that matter, how do you expect to support yourself there without . . . a diploma? Don't forget that high-school graduates consider themselves lucky if they can get a job just sweeping streets over there!"

"Excuse me, Monsieur, don't you think that if I had a fellowship, I could . . . ."

"A fellowship! But at present you don't have any diploma that would justify our making further efforts on your behalf, and besides you are obviously too old to be still enrolled in school! No one in France would accept you into secondary school! Do you know the age at which most people there complete the bachot?"*

" . . . ."

"Well, then, at the age of fifteen, my poor friend! Fifteen, sixteen!"

" . . . ."

"Figure it out for yourself! It's out of my hands, completely out of my hands, and besides, at your age I had already been the father of a baby girl for a long time! Oh, for a very long time!"

"Oh! Monsieur! I've always looked older than I am. People are quite big and strong in my family; take my father, for example . . . ."

"Even if you were, let's say, twenty years old, the funds at our disposal until the end of this fiscal year no longer suffice for us to . . . ."

"Oh! I'm sure I can pay for part of my trip; all I'm asking you is . . . ."

"But what will you do in France, where high school graduates sweep the streets? As for your admission into a lycée . . . ."

"But maybe it could be explained to the school superintendents over there that I am, I mean that I have the chance of becoming one of the first natives from this country to make . . . to continue on to the bachot, and that's the Good Lord's truth, Monsieur, because you know just as well as I do, Monsieur, that it is only since the last war, the recently concluded one of forty-five, that we too have been authorized to sit for the baccalaur . . . ."

I had the impression of having said too much. Truth has never been a staunch advocate for the poor devils of this world, and I sensed with great regret that my cause had been lost for good, when this high government official recoiled against the back of his armchair under the weight of my argument. What was I to do? Retract my statement, humiliate myself? But

---

*Abbreviation of "baccalauréat" (roughly equivalent to a high school diploma). (tr)

he had just deprived me of that opportunity by removing his hands from the table—those hands which, a second earlier, I would willingly have grasped and kissed with as much fervor as if they had been those of the mitered Goliath who was our formidable archbishop, a man who from time to time visited the minor seminary to pull our ears, utilizing them like the handles of a pot to raise us painfully from the ground when we were not sufficiently lucky to have him take hold of us by the lower jaw; as fanatical or depraved as we were at that time, we rejoiced that he was such a strong devil.

"Ah! Monsieur!" I blurted out with a sob in my voice, "That fellowship to study in France, I'm begging you for it on my knees!" But there wasn't enough room for me to transform words into actions; I limited myself to clasping my hands together and raising my eyes, glittering with passion, toward him as I plunged headlong into personal flattery that was sandwiched between two extravagant eulogies of France.

I stopped to take a breath, suspecting that it was not working, that Monsieur Dansette was not fooled, that all was lost; I began to fear that he would call the guard from the veranda and have me carted off to prison.

"I see, I see, my poor friend!" responded Monsieur Dansette impassively when I had finished. "First get to France," he added, rising skeptically to his feet. "Then finish your bachot! Well, we'll see if we can do something for you! But if you change your mind in the meantime, the Trade School run by Monsieur . . . ."

I stood up. It was six o'clock or six thirty. The extremely pale crescent moon, a sad parenthesis opening upon infinity, blurred in the darkness that descended from a brutal black sky and gradually became studded with the stars of the city's lights. Cars passed by; after having swept across me with its twin beacons of light, one of them drew up next to me.

I recognized a jovial Bendjanga-Boy in a soft felt hat—he was drunk— a cigar swelling one corner of his mouth as he lounged self-importantly in the back seat of a Pontiac and opened the door for me.

"Go!" he commanded the driver, exhaling a cloud of smoke.

Seeing the expression on my face, his smile froze. Suspecting that I might not be in the mood for a party, he burst into a volley of obscene curses and, planting his elbow on my liver, overwhelmed me with the alcoholic fumes on his breath (I unobtrusively turned my head to the side) before muttering, "zish old buggy!" He paused for a moment to lecture the driver, who seemed to be slowing down. "I wantsh to move fer ma money! Whatsha matta wit yuh, all shtiffed up to lishen wit yer bat's earsh to what we been shaying?"

"Massa!"

"No Masha here, yuh shtop when I tellsh yuh to shtop!"

The driver's back having bent over the steering wheel as soon as he accelerated, Bendjanga-Boy leaned over me for a second time, increasing the pressure of his elbow on my liver . . . .

Time passed. He sighed, then started talking again, as if to himself. "Ish only fer ze two uv ush. I sezsh ta my shef—before ze little one leavsh"—his voice faltered—"we gotta have one lash drink togezer, yuh never knowsh! Life ishn't anyzing at all, I sezsh; ish like a oil lamp, I sezsh. One little puff uv wind an' . . . ."

He hummed a motif from the Requiem in the back of his throat; it was a hoarse, muted melody that sounded like a death rattle. He choked, coughed.

"You're dead drunk," I told him.

"No, no, ish only zat I zought we gotta have shome fun like reshpec-table folksh and grand gentlemensh, no? We got zis old buggy, an' ish not in any nigger ash-hole bar where I wantsh to take yuh . . . . Ah, now I gotta tell yuh: ish true zat zere's one. I shaw it; zat's where we'll go!"

Before I had made the slightest hint of a movement, I found myself shivering at the cold, sticky, slug-like touch of his moist lips resting on the lobe of my ear and whispering, "to zeir club!" My interest in his proposal was heightened only by the possessive pronoun, since I had long ago foreseen the logical outcome of his inebriated state; in any case, I was quite unable to interrupt him, his elbow having rigorously curbed my body's involuntary start by pressing more firmly against my liver.

"Lil one!" he observed in a whining tone of voice, as if speaking to himself. "Yearsh an' yearsh we been lookin' at zem like we looksh at ze moon . . . . I knowsh people zat have died from zat kind uv hunger . . . . Oh, I might uv gone to zeir country during ze war, but . . ."

He raised his arm, and then let if fall with a despondant gesture in an arc inscribed by the glowing ember on the tip of the cigar.

". . . It wash too far . . . ." Then, abruptly changing his tone of voice: "my little idea wash to make zem take us fer reshpectable folksh, an' fer zat yuh gotta arrive in a lil old buggy, like grand gentlemensh or minish-tersh, eh . . . !"

He rubbed his hands together, and I experienced a sense of relief as his elbow left the vicinity of my liver and Bendjanga-Boy himself began to jerk about as if he were sitting on a nest of bedbugs.

"Yuh'll shee, lil one! Women like antilopesh in ze rainy sheashon, I shez ta yuh. Yuh knows, ze ones who cut yuh off in ze high grash jush behin' ze housh, ze ones wish zeir eyes zat go on forever, zeir rumps an' zeir breashtsh like people would shay zey wash made pregnant by ze rain. An' all zat wish electric lightsh, an' good wine, an' Tino shinging away. Ish like I got red pepper all over my body . . . only jush by thinkin' about it from ze other shide uv ze window . . . ."

He burst into laughter.

"Don't worry 'bout cash." He patted his briefcase . . . .

"Dreva!"*

"Massa!"

"Well zen, ish like I tol' yuh: yuh give a loud honk uv ze horn when we arrive!"

I was so weary and sick at heart that I no longer even reacted. What good would it do? Everything was over for me now that I had just lost my last chance for a trip to France. Until then, the hope of making this trip had been the most important motivation in my life. At present I no longer loved life enough to anticipate difficulties and potential catastrophes; on the contrary, I wouldn't have made the slightest effort to save myself, if our car had headed straight for the palm trees on the side of the road . . . .

"We're there, Massa!" exclaimed the driver, and he performed his task.

---

*"Driver" in pidgin.

Fifteen

By the stupor which greeted us, I sensed that we had arrived; it was unbearable—never before had the mere act of "existing" caused me such a shock. And yet, I had never lacked an awareness of it in the past. Nor was I living so absorbed in some blissful dream state as to become totally incapable of knowing my "self" under certain circumstances; quite the contrary, it was more of a banal, everyday fact, ceaselessly plotting the course of my black life since childhood, to the point that, if it ever accidentally abandoned its post, I was left with the impression of being frustrated and depersonalized in my tragi-comic relations with the Europeans into whose company my destiny as a so-called "man of color" had thrust me . . . . Which is not to say that some masochistic resolve had impelled me to coil up in a sanctum of bitterness, where I would spend my days telling the beads of a rosary and tirelessly mumbling, "I am a black man! I am a black man!" But the powerful revelation which I experienced upon entering this European night club, where people only tolerated those "half-whites"* who, when they perceived us, instinctively covered their faces with their hands, as if to protect themselves against our impertinent Negritude on these premises where they had perhaps been allowed to forget that they were black—this revelation stemmed largely from the electric, anguished silence to which our black and unwonted appearance had given rise. It was as if we had suddenly suspended time, light, and that murmurous clamor of party-goers absorbed in their carousels, all the customers having fallen silent, as if upon command, and remaining half turned toward the door, gestures frozen in the positions they had adopted

---

*The term "blanc-couillon" was used by the people of south-central Cameroon in referring to fellow blacks who had acquired the status of "French citizen" before the Second World War, although it had originally been applied to West Indian civil servants in Africa.

at the moment of our intrusion into their revelry, and all those round eyes leveled at us, those multi-colored eyes whose unpleasant lucidity swept through our souls, eyes immobilized in a steely glint of indignation that disconcerted us with anxiety. My entire body was trembling in spite of myself, although I made every effort to appear calm, pressing my thumbs tightly into the palms of my hands . . . .

A man was leaning on his elbows at the bar, and, prompted by a barely perceptible nod of his bald head, gleaming like a stone used for crushing ground nuts, a middle-aged little woman with the face of Charles the Fifth came to life between the telephone and the adding machine. Having lifted herself from her large stool, she passed around the bar, skirting it first on the inside and then on the outside, to invite us, although dispensing with her cheerful commercial smile, to please be seated at a free table in the back of the room; she pointed it out by raising her arm and thereby revealing an ample tuft of black matted hair protruding from her narrow armpit. The arm itself was gaunt and swollen at the elbow, where a thin diaphonous layer of skin, like a brightly transluscent film, enabled one to surmise the outline of the foetal heads of bones that seemed poised to pierce through it at the least false movement; I shuddered, fearing that something like that could very well happen to her as soon as she lowered her arm, which she still held in the air, slightly bent and with the monstrous elbow attached firmly to her side, while she scrutinized the motionless room, her razor-sharp bust wagging from right to left and occasionally giving a little jump, as if afflicted with a spasm or tic. It was precisely at this moment that two elderly native servants—covered with sweat and quite out of breath as they, for the first time in their career, remarked our sort of seedy-looking mongrel venturing ingenuously into this eminently respectable establishment which, except for the half-whites, tolerated only their own ancillary presence—shot through a red-curtained side door, white towels swinging from their forearms and with tragic, vengeful expressions on their faces. If the woman had not reassured us beforehand by indicating our seats to us, we would have thought that these powerful "boys," seething with rage, were mounting a charge against us, like myrmidons descending upon a helpless but headstrong victim. We crossed the room stiffly, our heads on fire, the ringing in our ears unpleasantly magnifying the muffled sound of our footsteps on the plaited rush mats. I was perspiring, for it seemed to me that the slightest gesture possessed an enormous potential for triggering unforeseeable consequences, and in a single movement, I finally sat down in a chair that one of the "boys" attending to us had brusquely pulled out for me. As soon as we had installed ourselves, the rainbow-colored room timidly regained a certain animation that our presence seemed to inhibit, as if we had inflicted a palpable sense of mourning upon the festive guests, who were reduced to communicating with each other in funereal and affectedly solemn whispers. Having sunk into a compliant prostration of our thoughts and senses, we were neither hungry nor thirsty, and it was with a lack of appetite that we listened to the monotonous cacophany of the knives and forks.

The man with the dazzling baldness, which was girdled around the base between his protruding ears by a modest iron-grey crown of carefully groomed hair, must have been the owner, and he sponged his face with little patting motions as he held an animated colloquy with his two servants and the woman with the face of Charles the Fifth before coming over to honor us with a speech that reeked of garlic, lavender, whiskey, and white tobacco. He spoke very softly, stammering, spluttering with impatience and anxiety; the poor man's sun-baked face beaded with sweat, turning alternately red and green as he interrogated what appeared to be the mute skepticism we were flaunting but which was, in actuality, nothing more than the congealed terror on our faces, although he undoubtedly interpreted it as the impregnable disdain of a death weighed and accepted in advance—the customary appanage of terrorists—and as if attempting to inspire us with more sanguine convictions, to save his business, and to gain time while awaiting the arrival of the police, he betrayed himself: "It's you or them; what do you want me to do about it? Me, I got nothin' to do with politics. You or them, it won't pay my taxes for me! Me, I'm no more than a poor white! Only, you know, it's them who earns me a living, so . . . ."

I made the hint of a movement to stand up.

"No, not at all!" he said, lowering his damp feverish hand onto my shoulder. "You shall be served!"

I shuddered in the foreboding that some ominous surprise might be in store for us and that the prospect of it was causing the owner to perspire in advance. He again mopped his face.

"What's he talking about?" inquired Bendjanga-Boy.

I translated.

"Good!" he exclaimed in French before finishing his sentence in our language, "let them serve us then! You only live once!"

Seeing how he was already making himself comfortable in his ignorance, I suddenly had a vague premonition.

"What's he saying, your companion there—your father, I suppose?"

The owner smiled, mopped the nape of his neck, and although neither of us had expressed our desire for it, he flung the command "two whiskeys" in the direction of the "boys," whose eyes continued to roll with astonishment under their own momentum. They twirled around in unison and marched, military fashion, toward the bar.

What occurred after this moment in Bendjanga-Boy's mind? Did he think that, the ice having been broken, the propitious moment had arrived for him to inform the owner of the real reason behind our intrusion, or was it the pretty smile of the woman who had just come down from the second floor in a tight-fitting skirt with a long slit on the side? In any case, despite my desperate, exaggerated gestures and my kicks under the table, an imperturbable Bendjanga-Boy motioned more menacingly than politely with his finger to the owner, who had left to reprimand the lady. When he returned, Bendjanga-Boy waggishly placed his outstretched lips into the hollow of the white man's ear; the latter was hardly reassured, and when he didn't seem to understand, Bendjanga-Boy adopted the sly, guilty look of an assassin, slowly pulled out his scarf, and spread it upon the table in front of the owner, who was alternately nonplussed, indignant, and furious. A rush of blood colored his bald head and then quickly subsided. The owner glanced around the room and pivoted on his heels with a violent backward movement of his upper body, knocking over tables and chairs in the process. Teardrops of our whiskey pursued a tortuous course across the oilcloth on the table. The "boys" came running. They grabbed each of us by the collar and the back of our pants.

"I didn't say anything, not me!" I protested. "It was him! He's not my father!"

"I'll give you brothels, sure I will!" roared the owner as he lent a helping hand to his servants, who were pushing us toward the door. He went back and forth between them, shouting, "I'll give you plenty of brothels!"

"Me senetah!" lied Bendjanga-Boy. "Me senetah! Me Ministah!"

"I'll give 'em to you, sure I will!"

"Get rid of this trash for me!"

They swung us into the darkness from the top of five or six stairs, and we landed on the refuse bins.

"I'll give 'em to you, sure I will! Apes!" The owner continued to shout, gesticulating wildly between his two "boys," who were conspicuously brushing their hands together in the illuminated rectangle of the doorway.

"Hey! Don't let them go!" yelled someone.

Preceded by the "boys," several Europeans shot from the interior and rushed down the stairs like blind men. Having appeared in their wake, the woman with the face of Charles the Fifth lit up the shadows with a luminous flashlight beam that began to scour the darkness. I had fallen just next to the wall, and the spear of light flitted over my head, probing as far as the piles of stones and sacks of cement beside the foundation of a half-finished house and causing parked cars to loom out of the shadows along with hibiscus hedges, a road, the drainage ditches, a cat that jumped into the shadows . . . .

"Over here! No, over there! On your right! They're not far away!"

The spear of light followed the voices.

"In the United States, they would have been lynched without any further ado!"

"Why were they allowed to leave?"

"They should have been punished first, and for that, all we had to do was invite the ladies to leave . . . ."

"Just think! Over here with the light!"

"Something's moving; something stirred on this side!"

"Where's that?"

"Next to the wall . . . . Point the light at the foot of the stairs."

I took to my heels and began running so quickly that I barely heard the crystalline tinkle of the coins I was sowing into the night. They chased me for nearly a kilometer; then, silence swallowed the galloping footsteps, the shouts, the insults . . .

That was the night I lost Isidore Bendjanga-Boy. I would never see him again. It was only a year later in Paris that I learned of his, if my mother is to be believed, "pious death."

"He died in peace!" At these words, which she had undoubtedly borrowed from Father D——, I once again saw him, the missionary, emerging from some smoke-filled shanty toward which he had trotted ponderously in his cassock, like a goat, which he favored by virtue of his little goatee, his profile, the jerky forward movements of his short, stocky, broad-shouldered torso as he walked, and especially his hoarse, nasal bleat in pronouncing "Dominus vobiscum" each time he was ritually obliged to turn his face toward the people and intone something soporific that he sanctified with the halo of his arms wallowing in the silky scallops of embroidery on his alb . . . .

They must have run in search of him at the first hint of a death rattle in Bendjanga-Boy's throat, and he had not responded until after having assured himself—his suspicious forefinger skating meticulously across the pages of an account book—that the dying man had faithfully discharged the annual tithe of the church-Sesame, upon the verification of which he ran to "bring him the Savior."

As for me, I continued my headlong course to the southern limits of the city, having aimed during the final two or three kilometers for a bowl of light that breached the darkness. "It's only the Spiritual Renaissance!" a group of young people informed me, turning around after having been alerted to my presence by my rapid breathing and the gusts of wind occasioned by my arrival. "Another of the white man's fads. All a person has to do is talk out loud about his sins in front of everybody. They love that. You see our fellow countrymen over there behind the white table? They've confessed their sins so well that they've been sent all over Asia and America just for doing that!"

Europe! My heart began to pound. I distanced myself from the crowd to recover my composure and leaned against a wall, reflecting that I finally had my chance! I approached and listened above the crowd to the confession of a woman. But she had absolutely no talent as a storyteller. I caught a glimpse of the well-fed niggers behind the table; I was going to amaze that screaming crowd with my story. What a novel my life! Spiritual Renaissance! I smiled and, with a beatific expression on my face, walked into the crowd, which opened spontaneously before me; as soon as I saw myself being approached by one of the four white men who had organized the meeting (the one whose face was so distended that he gave the impression of being on the verge of spewing forth something), the first sentence that was going to put me on the road to Europe came into my mind . . . .

THE END